# 'COMMUNITY'

*in the Writings of Jurgen Moltmann
for an Indian Ecclesiology*

# 'COMMUNITY'

## in the Writings of Jurgen Moltmann for an Indian Ecclesiology

**Godson Jacob**

## 2018

'Community' in the Writings of Jurgen Moltmann for an Indian Ecclesiology - Published by the Rev. Dr. Ashish Amos of the Indian Society for Promoting Christian Knowledge (ISPCK), Post Box 1585, Kashmere Gate, Delhi-110006.

Online Order: http://ispck.org.in/book.php

ISBN: 978-81-8465-???-?

Laser typeset by

ISPCK, Post Box 1585, 1654, Madarsa Road, Kashmere Gate, Delhi-110006 • Tel: 23866323

e-mail: ashish@ispck.org.in • ella@ispck.org.in
website: www.ispck.org.in

# Contents

# Acknowledgments

Firstly, I would like to thank God for blessing me the opportunity to work on this project. Having lived in the margins of ecclesial structures and rejection from conservative leadership, it is God who always pushed me to stride forward beyond every obstacle.

I would like to acknowledge the constant and consistent prayer of my mother Rachel Jacob and late father V. Jacob whose sacrifices and inspiration has emboldened theological pursuit.

I would like to express my appreciation to those who accompanied my journey of faith and for their courage to think differently. I am grateful to the Lutheran School of Theology at Chicago for their trust, support, and encouragement showed to me.

I am also thankful to my professor and advisor Dr. Jose David Rodriguez whose guidance helped in my academic engagement. His humility, persistence and academic brilliance have been a lighthouse for my academic and personal growth. Moreover, his presence and working with him as his teaching assistant for three years has imparted priceless wisdom for my future vocational and professional endeavors.

I also want to take this opportunity to thank Dr. K.G. Pothen whose guidance and suggestions helped me in shaping this work.

I also would like to mention Rev. Fr. Thomas Lamping for his help and encouragement in finetuning my theological thoughts through creative discussions.

# Foreword

Godson Jacob is an Indian born intellectual with a remarkable imagination, an extraordinary intelligence, and a clever ability to communicate. I've had the privilege of working together with him in his advanced program of studies, team teach various courses at the Lutheran School of Theology at Chicago, and learn from his knowledge and understanding in various areas of research. His diligence in providing the best critical appropriation of the intellectual production of South Asian (Indian) and Western scholarship, particularly in producing this interesting and well-argued study of the notion of community, shows his exemplary skills and abilities in scholarly work.

In his work, Godson lifts up his serious appreciation for interdisciplinary approaches of scholarship, as well as a profound understanding of the role of religion, and Christianity particularly, in responding to complex and demanding challenges of our time.

As a promising student who left his home town in India to venture into the Western World (Chicago, Illinois) in pursuit of a PhD relying on limited financial resources, Godson was forced to leave his family back home, to experience the challenges of a new world on his own. Moving forward in a strikingly new social and cultural environment Godson was challenged, as most people living in the diaspora are challenged, with building relationships from a position of great need. To be sure, he was accompanied in this endeavor with other international students in a comparable position; a center of theological studies eager to assist him in meeting this predicament, and a number of individuals who encouraged and supported him in this task. Surely, this experience must have led him to address this matter in one of his earliest formal writings.

His approach in writing this study is stimulating and thought provoking. Rather than just focusing on his former religious experience in India, he establishes a remarkable dialogue between his Indian background and the knowledge he has acquired while in the United States. He broadens his method to include a variety of areas of studies to bring a deeper understanding of his research topic. While his main interest seems to highlight the continuing relevance of religious knowledge, he is intentional in testing this religious wisdom in an open dialogue with culture, philosophy, the social sciences, interreligious dialogue in South Asia, Europe, as well as postcolonial historiography.

The chapters of the book increasingly open for us a wealth of valuable information about the topic. They enrich our personal ability to understand as well as address more pertinently the provoking present challenges of the notion of "community." For as the author claims, this is a concept "that escapes any one expert definition…" yet at the same time its understanding "becomes necessary in the context of religious fundamentalism, globalization and autocracy that incites a sense of communal aggression for one's own end and vacuum the essential function of community in the society." (p. 1)

As my task in this forward is to recognize the book's value and encourage you to read it, I want to end with the following assertion made by the author at the end of his study, "The community fulfills the task of a midwife who patiently helps and mediates the world to receive the unfathomable love and pain poured out on us by God through his only son. And when received the moment is celebrated leaving behind all differences that have left separated for the last thousand of years." (p. 133). While the primary focus for the author in this research was to "emphasize the theological relevance of the concept of "Community," and draw the holistic picture of community for constructing an ecclesiology suited for the Indian context," (p. 129) the real accomplishment of his work challenges us to reconsider our understanding of this concept and faithfully commit ourselves to its practice.

**José David Rodríguez**

*Augustana Heritage Chair of Global Mission
and World Christianity
Professor, Systematic Theology
Lutheran School of Theology at Chicago*

'Community'

.

# Preface

For the students of theology and ecclesiology the title "Community" in the Writing of Jurgen Moltmann for an Indian Ecclesiology will be reminiscent of Stanley J. Grenz's renowned work *Theology for the Community of God* whose construction of the traditional theological themes was with special emphasis on God's plan of creation and the establishing God's Community. Since "Community" in this book follows a trail that is constructive in its approach from Grenz's, this book intends to evolve from systematic assimilation to a more creative and constructive ecclesial program. The author intends to challenge the readers to think outside the box while approaching the understanding of church and its evolution in relation to its context. The church as a community is not just about come-in-unity or "assembly of believers" but it also reflects an organic reality that is based on acceptance, celebration, diversity, equality, and friendship. Community in this sense is not stagnant but more of a creative concept that offers many imaginaries of being a church.

The inspiration of this book is from Jurgen Moltmann's understanding of church that is dynamic and organic.

Moltmann's ecclesiology springs from his intimate relationship with God encountered in the abyss of pain and pathos. His experience as a prisoner of war opened his idea on God, Jesus, Holy Spirit, and Church. These experiences elaborated on his nature and vocation of being Christian and it underlined the emergence of a church embedded in reconciliation, openness, and courage to exist. Hence, any talk on God and Jesus Christ is a talk on Church and its being in the world. Since an understanding of community rests on the dynamic activity in God, it paves the way for the church to engage dynamically in the text and context of the world. The purpose of *Sarvodaya* Church in India is such an attempt to explore the possibility of the church to exist alternatively.

The purpose of this work is not to offer a comprehensive presentation on ecclesiology, but instead, a constructive blueprint on the contextual re-imagination of the church as an open community that exists for the liberation of all. While this book intends to explore new panoramas of ecclesial identity and its relevance in particular context, it is also useful for the beginners in the field of ecclesiology. In the Indian context where the Christian church exists in minority, it has less access to theological training and practice as compared to other Western and European context. As a result, any ecclesial existence requires creativity and fluidity to make church's identity relevant and meaningful among other major religions. Hence, it is a challenge as well as an opportunity. Therefore, the idea of *Sarvodaya* church is an open invitation for the upliftment of all.

# Abbreviations

| | |
|---|---|
| SCM | Student Christian Movement |
| ISPCK | Indian Society for Promoting Christian Knowledge |
| OT | Old Testament |
| NT | New Testament |
| OM | Operation Mobilization |
| P | Priestly |
| IT | Information Technology |
| AIIMS | All India Institute of Medical Science |
| 2G | Second Generation |
| CAG | Comptroller and Auditor General |
| MGF | Mar Gregorios Foundation |
| Ex | Exodus |
| GDP | Gross Domestic Product |

'Community'

# Glossary

| | |
|---|---|
| *Communitas* | Community |
| *Zoon politicon* | Human being |
| *Wesenswille* | Natural will |
| *Kurwille* | Rational will |
| *Gemeinschaft* | Community of feeling |
| *Gesellschaft* | Society |
| *Poiesis* | Production or labour |
| *Praxis* | Action |
| *Sanatana Dharma* | Eternal religion |
| *Satsang* | Community |
| *Bhakti* | Devotion |
| *Dharma* | Duty |
| *Sangha* | Community |
| *Ummah* | Nurturer |
| *Ummah muslimah* | Community submissive to God |
| *Iftaar* | Festival of Muslims |
| *Quran* | Sacred Book of Islam |

'Community'

| | |
|---|---|
| *Jihad* | Holy War |
| *Qahal* | Assembly |
| *Yahad* | Single or Unique |
| *Soma* | Body |
| *Ecclesia* | Called out |
| *Vita contemplativa* | Contemplation |
| *Vita Activa* | Action |
| *Perichoresis* | Exchange of Divine energies |
| *Ecclesia Romana* | Roman Church |
| *Filioque* | And from the Son |
| *Kirche* | Church |
| *Sammlung* | Assembly |
| *Gememeinde* | Congregation |
| *Ut Unum sint* | That they may be one. |
| *Energia* | Energy |
| *Nama* | Name |
| *Rupa* | Shape |
| *Sarvodaya* | Rise of all |
| *Kuttukettu* | Friendship |
| *Ahimsa* | Non-violence |

## CHAPTER-1

# Meaning of Community

## Introduction

Community is a concept that escapes any one expert definition. The understanding of community becomes necessary in the context of religious fundamentalism, globalization and autocracy that incites a sense of communal aggression for one's own end and vacuum the essential function of community in the society. The modern liberal forces drenched by western enlightenment and urbanization though has brought unfathomable contribution to the evolution of civilizations but has paralyzed the vitality of community relation under the dock of self-centeredness. In the name of creating a value-based community it has jeopardized the value on which every community derives its meaning and marched on to the road of individualism. Even Church which is a community is not alien to the effect of these forces and knowingly or unknowingly has become a reckoning force in facilitating their ideology into the fabric of Christian community. A study of community might pave the way for revitalizing the community dimension that has lost under the clouds of structural evil and bring out how a new picture of community would enhance a more peaceful and meaningful world. This chapter begins with an effort to understand the meaning of community and analyse it from sociological, philosophical, anthropological and religio-cultural and theological tradition for getting a clear picture.

## The Importance of Community

Community is an existential and social fact which becomes a lived experience only in relation to fellow beings. Jurgen Moltmann opines that the bodily existence of human being always means a social existence.[1] This existence is based on communion and therefore is essential aspect of human existence. Relation within community is a primordial bond, which is absolutely necessary for the normal development of the individual. It is only in sociality that personhood can be developed, if it is not being perverted into egoistical individualism. Selfhood is as much molded, stimulated and fulfilled by the human community as the human community is rooted in the individual's positive self-identification, empathy and appreciation which unite them as groups.[2] Moltmann alludes, "If being a human implies that to live in communion under the auspices of human experiences, is to live as community with communitarian values. If people are to be able to live as persons- body and soul, they must discover the divine dignity of community and look for the future of community."[3] In other words, community becomes relevant only in the presence of its divine values that sustain it.

The basic form of this bond is seen in family, owing mainly

to the natural love that unifies parent and children. Family is regarded as a nursery of social virtues. The affective bond of union consists in love. All communities imply love not only in the concrete relationship among persons involved but also their common values and thus for common good. Cultural Anthropologist and Social Psychologists equally stress the relevance of affective bond in community living. Love implies deep respect for human dignity which is concretized in the community. The affection within the community caricatures a moral dimension which calls for moral responsibilities towards the member of each community and towards one another. As a moral member of such community, one is conscious of oneself as co-responsible for, and cooperating in the establishment of the order of social whole. The wholeness thus received is part of freedom. As Thibon says, "there is no freedom without community, or a true community without freedom.[4] It means that community is rooted in freedom and vice versa. Therefore, a community becomes relevant as it constitutes one's identity and implants a sense of belonging thereby participating in freedom for building a just and peaceful community. A precise definition would suffice to impress why community is so important.

## Definition of the term 'Community'

Community has been singled out as 'one of the key ideas of the social sciences.'[5] The etymology of the word 'community' shows that it is derived from the Latin word '*communitas*,' which has several connotations: 1. a body of people having common organization or interest or living in the same place under laws and regulations; 2. society at large, a state, or common wealth;

3. joint relationship or ownership; 4. a common character or commonness. [6] Basically, community refers to the people who reside in a territory within which all people are subject to the same laws and the word carries the connotation of commonality (sharedness) of interests and purposes.[7] According to Bogardus, "a community is a social group with some degree of 'we-feeling' and living in a given area." J.R. Eshlemen and B.G. Cashion defined it as "a collection of people within a geographic area among whom there is some degree of mutual identification, interdependence or organization of activities."[8] According to McIver and Page, "whenever the members of any group, small or large, live together in such a way that they share, not this not that particular interest, but the basic condition of a common life, we call that group a community."[9] For Leo F. Schnore, "Community as a localized population which is interdependent on a daily basis, which carries on highly generalized senses of activities in and through a set of institutions which provides on a day to day basis the full range of goods and services necessary for the continuity as social and economic entity."[10] Mathew Varghese figures out certain omission in the definition particularly the sharing of culture.[11] But Schnore omitted it knowingly because the sharing of single culture would be an utopian concept, for single community might carry diverse cultural elements, especially in the Indian context. Therefore, it is the commonality based on state, laws, interest, we-feeling, interdependence, sharing of goods and services that make up the community. The next section elaborates on the nature of community and figure out how these elements are reflected in various socio-cultural and

religious communities.

## Nature of Community

A community is a union of a special kind dependent upon various unifying bonds- ontological, teleological, affective, moral, and communicative.

## Ontological Bond

It is a kind of bond that is developed out of the family community. It is in the family that the very being of an individual is constructed. In other words, family acts as a cradle for the becoming of any being in the society. Here an individual grows up in the environment of family members and relatives. As a person, man requires for his full development a special condition that the family community alone can supply, owing mainly to the natural love that unifies parent and children. St Augustine following Cicero, points to the family community as indispensable for a fully human existence-the nursery of social virtues and especially of the correct notion of command and obedience in society.[12]

## Teleological Bond

It is a goal or purpose-based bond where the primary unifying objectives and values are given priority along with the freedom of choice. In this bond, friendship is the most significant form of community bond, since it considers the mutual esteem of the people with similar interest and mutual assistance. This form of friendship can be precisely seen in sex inspired love, as it is fulfilled in the community of marriage.[13] Another form of goal-oriented bond can be observed among the business groups where a set of relation is produced among employer-employee, partners in business that aim to produce maximum profit. But the bond is too elusive in the case of student-teacher relation where they orient themselves for a better academic pursuit but sometimes end up in a more affectionate relation.

## Affective Bond

The Affective bond of union consists in love. This is most obviously the essential bond of union in the family, both as naturally effective and as morally binding in consequence. All community implies love, and this is not only in the concrete relationship among the persons involved but also in their working of common values and thus for a common good. Aristotle and Thomas Aquinas included under the love of friendship all forms of love directed towards the good of others.[14] This attitude implies deep respect for human dignity and forms the basis for measuring truth or falsity in love itself.

## Moral Bond

In response of the ontological and teleological bonds of community that are manifested in human nature, the members of a community have moral responsibilities towards one another as well as towards the community as a whole. The intricate relation between one another creates a sense of responsibility and freedom due to him/her as a person.[15] One actively participates not only in structuring the community but also preserving the moral values without jeopardizing the freedom of individuals.

## Communicative Bond

The unifying bonds can only become effective when communication is carried out in a proper manner. Anthropologically speaking, there are human characteristics that make communication possible. They are traditions, human satisfaction, freedom and the knowledge of natural law. Every human society has traditions which are made alive through language, symbols, mini narratives etc. These traditions when communicated from generation to generation construct a more reliable culture of one's community. Communication through different arts, literature, science and technology reflects human desires and aspirations.[16] Thus it has been observed that the nature of community reflects certain bonds that are indispensable for the growth and nourishment of community. In order to get a more holistic picture of community, it becomes mandatory to pursue a deeper understanding of community from the perspective of social sciences.

## Sociological Perspective on Community
The succeeding section will try to situate community from different angles. Sociology is one such branch of science that can enlighten us and bring a more precise understanding.

## History of Concept
Ancient Greek philosophy termed the human being '*zoon politicon*,' a social being, who is dependent on others materially and physically, as well as spiritually and culturally. Only in the polis- in community with other people-can a man or woman find fulfillment.[17] The development of friendship was essential to this concept. According to Cicero, 'consensus in law as well as interest is the basis of community.'[18] John Rawls in his book

*The Theory of Justice* analyzed the primitive cultures which featured common good as the criterion of community.[19] The dichotomy between rational/legal and spiritual/emotional became the context of all subsequent attempts of definition. With the rise of Sociology, the above said dichotomy previously found in social philosophy was transmuted into the classification of social relation and social groups. Sociological research continues to employ both variations of the communal-associational typology and concepts of community as locality group. It is observed that accelerating urbanization and the concomitant impersonality and functional specificity of interaction in modern society have given preeminence to analytic rather than spatial concepts. Thus, it is obvious that the concept of community is not new but as old as the humanity itself.

## Theoretical Orientations

In continuing the work of systematic studies of communities, general sociologist and anthropologist of 1920s, Gunter Remmling provides with certain theoretical aspects of community. According to Gunter W. Remmling and Robert B. Campbell, at least four discernible orientations can be developed, such as social psychological emphasis, cultural emphasis, ecological emphasis and European theoretical orientation.[20]

## Sociological Psychological emphasis

The members could maintain close, continuous, personalized, face-to-face contacts. They could develop mutual identification with each other and the territory itself and thereby establish solidarity, unity or common interest.[21] All necessities of communal life could be obtained through locally institutionalized organization, which function as both the establishers and the enforcers of local norms.

## Cultural Emphasis

It sees community in the context of its being a localized, total culture bearer and the common point in the life of the society's member in which the broad culture becomes operative. The community in this sense is the interactive situation in which the broad cultural patterns are manifest.[22] To put it differently, community is the lantern of cultural manifestation. In the Indian context, culture is always expressed alongside religion, it is necessary to look into the religious emphasis on community, which will be discussed in the later section.

## Ecological emphasis

The main aspect discussed in this emphasis is the spatial distribution of human life forms as the sub-social basis and the limiting factor upon which community rests. People both as individuals and as types are conceived as functionaries who are naturally interdependent. Example: Regardless of their prejudices the farmer is dependant upon the urban men as his market and the producer of his tools and the urban men is dependent upon farmer for food and fiber.[23] These orientations are found substantiated in the functional analysis of community in relation to the society.

## European Theoretical Orientation

Although European orientation is not applicable for Indian context, however, it has to be analyzed because of its influence in the minds and ethos of Indian sub-continent. In the European circles, the community is seen as an association rather as a territorial group. Sociologists like Georg Simmel and Ferdinand Tonnies prefer to use 'communality' and 'functionality' rather than community to avoid confusion. It is because of the role-to-role pattern that dominates in the large cities. Though the small towns have the same kinds of institutionalized organization (church, school, business etc.) as do the cities, their modes and 'flavor' is somewhat different. The sociability and personal aspects are rendered irrelevant or impractical in the cities, largely because of sheer size and of the accessibility of 'competing' organizations.[24] In the present Indian context, the interpenetration of social and cultural values of Europe has made substantial inroads into the community values and replaced by a more role associated relation within the garb of urbanization. The reason why some of the Indian states still have strong communitarian relation unlike the European countries that bifurcates the secular with religion, is due to the harmonious existence of both secular and religion that brings the community together which can be witnessed during festivals. Various orientations have brought out the theoretical portrayal of community dynamics but there is a major missing link i.e. the overlapping in the understanding of interaction between community and society on a functional basis which will be clarified in the next section.

## Interaction between Community and Society

Human beings in general are divided into two: communities and societies. They are the two modes of social order and structure.[25] Ferdinand Tonnies employs two concepts *Gemeinschaft* and *Gesellschaft*. It is approximately translated as community and society respectively. He examines it by viewing the human volition of which he distinguished two types- *wesenswille* (natural will) and *kurwille* (rational will).[26] *Gemeinschaft* refers to the community of feeling that results from likeness and from shared life experiences. In them, individuals consider other individuals as ends in themselves, while they know each other personally, create strong emotional bonds through frequent face-to-face interaction and mutually participate in each other's lives. This action is based on natural will. *Gesellschaft* or society on the other hand, connotes a completely different setting where people live in a large, densely populated area; they have diverse values, roles and tradition. Their relation in public life is more on a contractual basis. This action is moreover on a rational will.[27] Here Tonnies has been criticized of giving a romanticized picture of the community which was seen in pre-industrial period (a homeliness feeling) in contrast to the industrial society marked by capitalism.[28] Let us venture into the interaction of modernization, which has led people to be more innovative and ambitious thereby fleeing to other cities for greener pasture and adapting itself to the community framework.

## Urbanization and Community

Change is an inevitable factor. So is also with the community. Large scale changes bring change in the community as well. In the study of sociology, urbanization brought a long-lasting change in the lives of communities. It emerged with industrialization. Urbanization has unquestionably contributed many positive things to modern life. Along with many gifts, it has produced evil innovation as well. Due to this, there has been constant tug of war between affluence and abject poverty in the urban life. Some opine that urbanization is detrimental to the existence of community causing its disintegration. One of the underlying factors of this disintegration is the heterogeneity (different people) that prevents the kind of interaction which characterizes community. Increased rate of unemployment due to the competitive nature and survival of the fittest technique leads one to crime. As a result, people become more self cautious leading to self-centeredness. Another suggestion is that community can persist within large societies. It does not destroy community, rather it open the space for the emergence of many communities like community of rich and famous, of beurocrats, of scientists and intellectuals, middle class and poor. These are situated like meter gauge train compartments without mutual doors fitted i.e. without any mutual relationship and friendship. Another perspective is that urbanization neither destroys nor allows it to persist but give rise to new communities.[29] It is a community that is based on common activities. For example, clubs, competitions, charity organizations etc. But this type of communities fades away as they lose people. As the people live in closed compartments, they escape the matrix of relationality which can be clearly observed in the changing of community sentiments.

## Changing Character of Community Sentiments

The Changes brought about by modernity also brought changes in the attitude and life-style of the people at large. It is observed that there is a shift from welfare community to interest-based community. While belonging to a particular community people are also a part of other communities or associations so that one's interest becomes specialized. With the strategic modification of science and technology, communication has enabled the individuals to go beyond the limits of one's community and enter into their own way of reaching to the top at any cost. Today people are often tended to look the greenery of other end of the line and consider their own communitarian values as dry straw. People are searching for an international community to make themselves fit with the international demands which can be witnessed in larger cities. It is therefore crucial, but difficult indeed, to learn to cope with the fact that in real life we have plurality of identities and loyalties which have to be accommodated on the basis of tolerance, horizontal connections and democratic process. It is the basis for nurturing mature human persons-in-communities.[30] Recently, there has been a turning away from the morphological approaches which conceive community in terms of a set of fixed and immutable characteristics, in favour of the view which regards community as existing in the minds of the people who experience and give meaning to it. It means that communities are 'constructed' or 'imagined.'[31] Therefore, our perception of community is an evolution from communal bonding based on love to how we imagine community based on experiences of one's reality.

## Philosophical Dimension of Community

The Sociological analysis of the community does not exhaust the depth of meaning inherent in the understanding of community. Therefore, it is necessary to avail the help of other social sciences particularly the philosophical aspect of community. The concept of community has got significant emphasis in the area of philosophy. A brief analysis of both Western and Eastern philosophical framework of community will be the touchstone of this segment. In pursuing the idea of community, how the human person is understood with its instinctual nature of human bonding. In other words, human person is always comprehended in terms of its nature of being relational.[32] Ontologically speaking, the element that makes community is the act of communion. It is this communion that makes our being. This ontological priority of the communion provides the basis for the necessity of philosophical analysis. It is understood that all community has the principle of having communal harmony and organic unity of humankind along with the nature. Human's ontic fulfillment rests on their belongingness to a single community of cosmos common to all. The Early Upanishad of India teaches, 'the cosmos is a single nest for mankind,' while Heraclites of Greece asserts, 'the waking have a single cosmos in common.'[33] All human being irrespective of what s/he is or what s/he does survive in the network of relationship and always show an adherence towards the community. All individual represents in itself the blueprint of a community. In other words, every individual follows a relational pattern not only outside of oneself but also in the inside i.e. different organs live in perfect harmony as a community to carry the bodily function in a holistic way. Just as an individual represents a community so also is a community a part of the wider cosmic community. One can say that the philosophy of community envisions a cosmic unity-one cosmos, one community.[34] Thus, community in communion can only flourish when it acts completely in unity with the whole cosmos.

The fuller development of the self is only possible within the community. It is real community or communion with other persons which transforms them from an 'it' into 'thou' or 'we,' no longer impersonal objects but real beings (*sat*), co-existence (*chit*) and co-ecstatic (*ananda*) according to the Upanishad.[35] Therefore, the aspirations of the community in the philosophical language affirms to live in unity and belongingness and participate in the cosmic community building thereby providing one's authentic self the will to exist. How does the relational aspect of community contribute to the society at large? Aristotle distinguishes basic human faculties, namely *poiesis* (production or labor, the foundation of household and of the economy), and *praxis* (action as intersubjective, exchange, foundation of politics).[36] For Aristotle the distinctiveness of *poiesis* and the verb *poieo* in contrast to *praxis* is that they designate an activity that results in the production of something entailing an objective result, while *praxis* conveys a deed done that has an intersubjective effect but does not result in a positive and material outcome.[37] Therefore community in its essential terms looks into the order of its household functions and participates in the well-being of the society at large through its action in unity and solidarity. The philosophical expression of inner dynamics of community like poiesis and praxis poses a separate platform explaining the function of community. This becomes relevant contribution in the writings of Jurgen Moltmann, which will be discussed in the next chapter.

## Lessons from Anthropology

Robert Redfield identifies four key qualities in community: a smallness of social scale; homogeneity of activities and state of mind of members; self-sufficiency across a broad range of needs and through time; and a consciousness of distinctiveness.[38] Traditional anthropologist approaches community in three different ways: i. common interest between people (Frakenbing 1961), ii. A common ecology and locality (Minar and Greer 1969), iii. A common social system or structure (Warner 1941). In short, it emphasizes on essential commonality as the logic underlying a community's origination and continuation.[39] Recently Anthropological studies have been concentrating more on the 'how' of community. In other words, how 'community' is elicited as a feature of social life; how membership of community is marked and attributed; how notions of community are given meaning. Anthony Cohen argues that community is a symbolic construct and a contrastive one i.e. awareness of community depends on consciousness of boundary. He says communities and their boundaries exist essentially not as a social structured system and institutions but as a world of meaning in the minds of their members i.e. symbols, signs and shared vocabulary of values.[40] The evolutionary approach in anthropological studies proposes social evolution in community. It means that the traditional, static, naturally developed forms of social organization such as kinship, friendship, neighborhood and folk, would everywhere be superseded by association expressly invented for the rational achievements of mutual goals. In other words, community was driven away from the emotional side to a commercial face of human existence characterized by capitalism and individualism. Whatever be the change in the idea of community, but its inherent nature brings the people together as a social-cultural grouping which will always fathom for a place where everyone wants to belong. This belongingness which is basic to an individual is also at the core of every religious and cultural tradition which binds a community together.

## Community in Religious and Cultural Traditions

A study on community cannot get exhausted by only looking into the social, philosophical and anthropological aspect because every individual in one way or the other are part of some kind of religious and cultural traditions. It is important to fathom the religious beliefs of the community that serves as a bond of communion among the members. Moreover, it is noteworthy that every religious tradition understands and interprets community differently. Therefore, it becomes an emergency to dig deeper into those understandings that every religious tradition confers on community.

## Community in Hinduism

Hinduism in essence is called as *Sanatana Dharma*-eternal religion and is followed by majority of people in India as a way of life without strict boundaries. It has been observed that Hinduism is not a handmaid of Aryan culture rather it is observed as an amalgamation of both pre-Aryan and Aryan religious traditions. As Chettimattam says, "a real dialogue took place between them and the outcome saved and integrated the positive elements of both religious cultures."[41] The purpose of the Aryans was to develop a community that should have a supremacy over the indigenous community. To facilitate their agenda caste system was introduced to promote a community with specific designation and distinctive role under the ladder of caste system. These distinctive roles were practiced under the banner of svadharma or personal duty. It is not dictated from outside by an external authority, a written law or an abstract ideal, but rose from the very internal life of the sacral community. Here community stands as a source of morality for persons to carry out their responsibilities. But this community based on caste system has been largely criticized due to its stratification and the consequent form of injustices practiced in the system. The social status of each caste is strictly fixed and solidified under the old traditional system. It became an iron fist in the hands of the rich to crush the poor and the Dalits. Today this form of caste-based community has been complemented by the globalization and capitalism.

The emergence of Hindutva is another force that caters an ideology to bring everyone under their supremacy. The person in a community is not understood by traditional Hinduism in an individualistic way. The essence of a person is relationality with a deep association with the fellow beings and the divine.[42] Apart from the community based on caste system, there are other sublime forms of community existing in Hinduism. One of such forms can be traced in the existence of *Satsang* which is derived from the two Sanskrit words 'sat' means 'true' and 'sang' means 'community.' It is an ashram life regulated by the rule of love in worshipful service (*Bhakti*) to be expressed by constant bhajans.[43] This community is characterized by mutual love, equality and service. It emerged along with the bhakti tradition. The examples of Kabirdas and Tulsidas which shows this attitude transcend all caste barriers and voiced for a community based on equality. The emergence of renascent Hinduism has put a spark in the hearts of the people to fight for their rights. They pursue for a just community that is unscathed by evil forces of society. Dalit Panthers' liberation movement is one such movement that searches for an ideology of a new humanity for a new community. In short, despite the casteist structure of Hindu community, there are other love and equality-oriented community like *Satsang* in Hinduism that runs contrary to its casteist legacy.

## Community in Buddhism

In the history of religious tradition, it has been reasoned that Buddhism came as a protest religion against the Brahmanical authority and ritualistic religion of Vedic period. It challenged the Vedic authority and declined to worship their gods. It was in the context of highly stratified society based on caste that put people under the service of high caste Brahmins. The people belonging to the lower section of the society were not admitted into the mainstream of the community life. In such a time of discrimination and segregation Buddhism offered an alternate community. Buddhism admitted into their religious communion all people, irrespective of caste and class, which was a direct opposition to the supremacy of the Brahmanical system. It emerged as revolution of the common people against the privileged nobles.[44] Three principles can be traced in Buddhism: trust in Buddha, *Dharma* and *Sangha* or community. In the Buddhist monastic order, the word 'Sangha' comes from Sanskrit word referring to the gathering of the tribal republics of the time.[45] It is a kind of facilitating social organization that keeps their community protected and enriching.[46]

The intention of Buddha's discipline was to create an ideal community conducive for spiritual growth. This community was not a projection of particular doctrines rather a social community guided by rules with soteriological objective characterized by shared experience, that led to become a religious community.[47] He also opted for a local Sangha so that people can take care of oneself in a more consensual basis.[48] The values that the community reflected was self-reliance and involve in work which would help one in satisfying one's needs. The scripture of this religion contains sections that provide training codes for monks and nuns to live a life of meditation and nurture monastic life. The Sangha supports its members by solidarity, example, teaching, mutual acknowledgement of digression....[49] It is a community of equality without distinction in ranks and position in the decision making. Again, the intention of community was to break from the traditional community to a more inclusive community, but it has itself ended up in an isolated and separated community from the society. It only focused on the cleansing of oneself and the community failing to make an impact in the evils of the society.

## Community in Islam

Community in the understanding of Islam is very crucial and carries the essence of one's life.[50] The word used for community in Arabic is '*Ummah*' derived from 'um' means 'mother'; 'nurturer.' It means that community provides motherly care and nurture believers' life. It is like a child which cannot survive without its mother, so also with the believers without community. It has often referred to the unity of Muslims throughout the world. It has got religious connotations. The ideal of an *ummah muslimah*, a unified, just, and pious "community submissive to God," is central to the Islamic religious vision. Abraham prayed that his posterity would be such a community (surah 2:127-129), and Muhammad shared Abraham's vision in establishing his *ummah*. The foundations, boundaries, and character of this ummah as a religious and political entity were fixed in the first few centuries of Islamic history, with the *ummah* from the time of the Prophet and the first four caliphs as the normative embodiment of the ummah ideal.[51] It also represents the people who are the chosen vessel of God to carry God's plan. The *Hadith* literature defines *Ummah* as a kind of social unity that provides identity to its adherents.[52] The basic characteristics of Islamic community are sharing and unity in diversity. It can be rightly observed in the celebration of *Iftaar* by the Muslims worldwide. It means the breaking of fast. *Iftaar* binds the community together by sharing of the eatables from different neighbourhood. The concept of unity of God in Islam leads ultimately to the unity of whole mankind which is well portrayed in this celebration. It is guided by moral values of *Quran* which plays the central role in the formation of Muslim community and shaped its tradition and history.[53] All the religion including Islam opts for the liberation of humankind from the clutches of poverty, exploitation, social and economic injustices. It is these elements that can make a community worthwhile. But today this sharing is intended to patch up political ties for political motives. M. Hasan in his article in *The Hindu* newspaper analyses the other side of the present Islamic celebration. Politicians hold *Iftaar* parties not with a heart to experience fellowship but to better the vote-bank for the forthcoming election. He alludes, 'Investment in such fellowship 'improves' political image, bringing electoral returns.[54] Thus, it is observed that a sincere festivity which is only aimed at community fellowship has been taken to perform political gimmick for the survival of political community. It has also led to the formation of community that misinterprets and incites the youth to take radical action and avenge those who are against their community which they call *jihad*.

## Community in Primal Religions

It is interesting to note that the above said religions has their community understanding from the written documents of the past leaders or scholars but the notion of community in primal religions has not come from any religious documents or from religious teaches but as a way of life reflected in the community itself. It is the very life of the community that provides the basics of community building and its sustenance. For a tribal, life is a unity. There is no distinction between the secular and the sacred, physical and spiritual, earthly and heavenly.[55] This holistic vision of an undifferentiated unity is the essence of tribal culture. It is a kind of organic union with a symbiotic life.

Panger Imchen gives some aspect that portrays the organic unity among the primal communities. First is the blood relation that endows with the binding of family, villages and tribes together. This raises the sense of belongingness caricatured by trust. They also have communion with the dead ancestors whom they feel as the guide of the community from every kind of evil. Secondly, they live in harmony with nature. To phrase it differently, the community does not just think of its own survival but also treat nature as part of their community fulfillment. Thirdly, land plays a major role in their life because it is the source of sustenance, nourishment, support and identity. The land does not provide any marked rules but a rule that is egalitarian and democratic in function which thereby encourages the individuals to live in a community. There is no landless person and family. The land is equally distributed to all the families of the clan from the beginning.[56] Thus community has a significant role in Primal religion. It negates the individualistic thrust of the modern societies. It provides proper place for persons in the community. It enhances an integral and holistic relationship between humans, fellow beings, universe and the Supreme Being. Thus, Primal religions focus more on the cosmic definition of community. In the primal religion the importance of community is strong enough to sacrifice any individual for the good of the community without taking adequate step to improve the quality life of the individual by offering another chance. Their notion of community is not to possess the humanitarian life in its inclusiveness but to uphold the community's interest only.

## Community in Judeo-Christian Tradition

The aforementioned aspect of community from different religious tradition has put pressure to unravel the meaning of community in the Judeo-Christian tradition. In this tradition the resources for finding the meaning of community comes from the Biblical literature that has landed from the experiences of varied community life. Bible portrays the story of a community that had been chosen by God to carry out God's will on earth. It has been inferred that there might be some overlapping in the essential characteristic of other religious notion with that of Judeo-Christian tradition, but the anticipation is made due to some unique features on community available in the Biblical tradition. A close scrutiny on the tradition would enlighten us more in the knowledge of community.

## Biblical Notion on Community

Community has occupied a central stage in the Bible. It talks about a God who creates humankind so that he may relate and have communion with his creation. Here communion is the very nature of God. Gen 2:18 says, 'it is not good for the man to be alone,' depicts God's intention for human to have communion.[57] As Julio Sabanes says that God wants to draw us out of our isolation and egocentrism and to bring us into a community of love.[58] There are some elements in both Old Testament and New Testament that need to be analyzed for a better understanding of community.

Old Testament Vision

The concept of community plays a major role in the history of Jewish culture and tradition.[59] It is their belief that the call of Abraham was the beginning of a new community started under the auspices of God. The continuing affect can be seen in the deliverance/liberation of Israelites out of the Egypt.[60] It was this belief that made them into a community, a society bound to each other and to God by a covenant which was the response to his great act of deliverance. In OT, two words are used directly referring to community. They are *qahal* and *Yahad*. The word *qahal* denotes 'assembly,' or 'assembled group of people.' It refers to the cultic community, which can be seen in Deutronomistic tradition, Psalter, in P and in Chronicler history.[61] The word *qahal* is used, since the monarchic era, for a legal community with firm demarcated membership which exclude any gentiles and those with gentile imperfection (Proverbs 5:14; 26:26). In the Chronicler history, the word is used for assembled political nobility (Deut. 17:8) along with religious overtones.[62] The essence of the word stands for a community dimension of the existence of the people of God without any gender bias. They were community of Yahweh that means they owed their allegiance to Yahweh and at the same time bound with their fellow beings. The term *Yahad* mean as 'one, single or unique.' It is in fact 'one': as a verb 'be one'; as a noun 'unity' or 'entirety.'[63] Along with all these meanings, the use of the root suggests that such community also involves association with God. Thus, there is both social solidarity and theological affirmation. The question is what sort of community was God intending for Israelites?

God's deliverance of Israelites out of Egypt was to continue the covenant relationship started with Abraham. It was the covenant community that God was forming. The term covenant (berith) shows a fresh experience in the life of Israelites with God and God's experience with his people.[64] The responses of God within the covenanted relationship are related to the responses of man to his claim upon him.[65] The covenant formulae in Ex. 6:7a does not envisage an individual but a community.[66] As Mowinckel also asserts, "the basic reality in Human life, for the Israelites, not the individual, but the community. The individual has his real existence in the tribe. Outside of that he was nothing, a severed member, one without rights."[67] Here the thrust on community does not ward off the importance of individual rather it is affirmed because it is the individual that constitutes the community. It is the ideological preferences on individual needs which is to be avoided. In other words, individualism can hamper the smoothness of a community. Even the calling of Abraham and establishment of covenant should not be seen in terms of priority given to an individual rather it was for the whole community. Fretheim says, 'Abraham was just a part of the covenant for a future community.[68] Abraham became the stepping stone towards a covenanted community.

During the time of prophets, we see God's oracles coming out of the prophet's mouth with a sole purpose of making the community of Israel realize the need of recalling the basic law of community. The oracles were the result of the failure from the sides of Israelites to live as a community. Their failure was not in the forgetfulness of their religious practices, but it was rather in their disregard of the economic laws that bound them together as a chosen people.[69] Thus it is clear that OT view the community not only in terms of showing Israelites as God's chosen people but also to enhance the people of Israel to live as a community with all its socio-economic worth. Thus, Israel as a community with a sense of solidarity generally was given an additional sense of solidarity and religious bondedness through the covenant. Along with the filial relationship, a common experience of Exodus was added which together became the substrate of forming a covenant people.

## New Testament Vision

Some of these understanding continue the legacy of OT into the New Testament. Jesus and early Christian themselves believed this aspect and interpreted community in the light of their ministerial function. The presence of community can be traced back to Jesus' calling of disciples. His preaching of the Kingdom of God was intended to raise a community who would gather together in God's name and worship him. For him, community was a place of God's presence. He says, "where two or three are gathered together in my name, there am I in their midst (Matt 18:20).[70] Jesus was always seen along with a group of people because those people were decisively influenced by their conviction that Jesus was God's messiah. Through him, God has begun a new exodus for the restored, eschatological Israel i.e. a new community of Jesus Christ. It would be wrong to say that Jesus was only concerned about community and leaving away the individual position in the community. Jesus' concern for the community starts from his ministry to the individuals (Matt 8:1-4; 9:1-8Mk 7:24-30 etc.), but with a view towards the building of community. As Guthrie notes that Jesus' always upheld the view that God's concerns always for community first rather than some individual.[71] His ministry to the sick, poor and needy, was based on bringing them back to the community of God's Kingdom (Matt 11:4ff). This attitude can be observed in the Sermon on the Mount, where he provides some qualification to enter into the Kingdom of God. One must be merciful to others (Matt 5:7); be a peacemaker (v9) etc. These criteria are kept by Jesus to give thrust on one's responsibility as a human for others in the community. Also, Jesus' ministry was not only about bringing people to the Kingdom of God but also to bring God into the hearts of his people. Robert Wall opines that Jesus wanted his community to be centered on God.[72] This led his people from self-centeredness to God-centeredness. It implies that becoming a member of the messianic community which has the signs and token of the coming Kingdom.[73]

The saying of Jesus for his community goes in line with OT idea of covenant community. Just as the covenant community live together in unity and belongingness so is the community of Jesus live in friendship and fellowship. This community represents essence of family where all are bonded together in love. It is a family where all are equal in the eyes of God. It is a mosaic family that takes into account the feelings of other without any biased attitude. It was these qualities that attracted people from different walks of life to the community of Jesus. This community relation was carried in the early Christian period and became a reality. Some problems creeping in the community called Church made Paul to respond to the need of interpreting the sense of community for establishing a better Church.

The Early Christian community followed the path of Jesus Christ, which was characterized by selfless service. Among the early Christians, it was Paul who offered a systematic theological understanding of community. He took the metaphor of 'body of Christ' to relate Christ's death and resurrection to his understanding of the church as the community of believers who partake in it. Why does Paul use the metaphor 'body' to explain about community? When Paul calls the church a 'body'-Greek *soma*, he always means a living body, or 'the external presence of the whole man.'[74] Paul connects the body with community in terms of its holistic function. Just as the body functions only in relation to function of all the organs together, so also with the community operates in relation to the unity of members in the community. Therefore, the body of Christ represents the body of a new community, marked out in Christ. Paul uses the term *ecclesia* to denote the body (Eph1:22; Col 1:18, 24). This new community in Christ is the radical 'new creation' of God on Christ (2Cori5:17). Eschatologically, the new creation means a transformed community with no ultimate separation between human and human; God and human.[75] From an ecclesial perspective, the community created by Christ was to establish the relation between God and human. It means that a true community not only looks forward for the reunion of humanity, but it also caters to the need of reuniting God and human.

For Paul, the principle that guides the life of the faithful was the principle of the Spirit of Christ that constituted the body of equals before God at the same time as they remained divergent in the gifts they had to offer.[76] It implies that the members that constitute community are also constituted with different gifts for the edification of the community. No individual with their respective gifts can claim superiority within the community because it is God who has delivered it for the well-being of the community. The Eucharistic meal is the prime symbol of the unity and equality of all individuals. In this communion, the community participates not only for themselves but with a vision to go outside of the community and become a witness in the world. Jesus mission was to serve the people irrespective of who s/he was in their orientation. In the same way the motive of the community should not be restricted to itself rather witness the love of Christ for the whole world (Rom12:9-20). In other words, the love of Christ is not to convert an individual and increase the quantity of the community rather imparting selfless commitment to the building of the Kingdom of God in the hearts of the people. Thus, Pauline community is also a witnessing community with a heart of service.

These religious traditions particularly Hinduism, Islam and Buddhism present a community that focus on pristine form of charity and thereby assuming a goodwill gesture leaving behind the spiritual role of the community in building a just society. To phrase it differently, it portrays an immanent character of a community. On the other hand, Judeo-Christian tradition provides more of a transcendental role of community that survives in relation to God. But Moltmann concept of community provides ample space to bring both the transcendental or spiritual and immanent or charity together in one knot.

## Theological perception of Community

It is inferred from different disciplines and traditions that community is a communion of group of people with similar interest participating in the well-being of each individual caricatured by the bond of love for God and for fellow beings. Church being one of the major aspects of theological enterprise prompts us to look into the necessity of theological rationale of community. A theological understanding of community becomes necessary because the dynamics of communion can be well observed in the Church, as Paul emphatically equates Church with that of redeemed community called out by God to witness the love of Christ for the people. Bible stands as a witness to the making of a community called out by God. Exodus event is the paradigmatic moment where a group of people move from their experience of alienation to that of a reconciled people of God. In this communion they are covenanted with God and with each other.[77] Further this people became a charismatic community which bears continuing effect of God's salvation- creating grace in its new life as an alternative to the norms and values of the social order.[78] There is also an essential dimension to the community. As John Zizioulas points that, "there is no true being without communion; Nothing exists as "individual," conceivable in itself. Communion is an ontological category."[79] This ontology arises out of their exploration of the mystery of Trinity, in which being itself is the result of communion of persons. This communion is realized in the Eucharistic meal which is instituted by Christ and constituted by Spirit. In short, God lives in communion and intents that humans should live as community. For Miroslav Volf opines that this would lead Zizioulas to "overrealized eschatology."[80]

In Pannenberg's term Church is an 'elected community' that participates to serve the people with a purpose of creating a fellowship of humanity.[81] A community can be called church when it accepts Christ as the head. It is the presence of Christ that makes the community of people called Church. It is Christ that binds the people together and imparts life into it. Just as Christ shared his life to his people through his love, the life of the Church members should be characterized by mutuality and sharing without any self-interest. These characteristics can only be achieved through the way of Christian discipleship. The aim of this discipleship is to establish right relation among believers and adherence to Christ. Also, Church as a community is not only for itself but exists for others around it. As Bonhoeffer says that Church is not only a community of saints but also communion of responsible people who hear and give themselves for others in the world.[82] Process thought observes that Church in its origin was a voluntary community in which interpersonal relations were experienced chiefly as liberating rather than restricting. People would think of themselves as members one of the other in the intimate way in which the parts of the body belong to one another. This community was based on new community of love and mutual participation.[83] Thus Church is a community of believers that witness the love of Christ, which is the shared interest of the community, take into account the need of the others outside of one's community without any individual priority.

## Conclusion

This chapter has enlightened us with different definition along with Sociological, Philosophical, Anthropological, Religio-cultural, Biblical and Theological perspectives on Community. This insight has clearly portrayed the indispensability of community in the path of human existence. Community helps not only the wellbeing of a group, but it also caters the needs for personal growth and survival. It is learned that community is not just a theoretical and abstract concept but something to be reckoned in one's life. The basis of community is relationality that is bonded in love. The form of this relationship may vary from place to place but it's essential dynamics will remain the same. But today, with the fast expansion of modernization and capitalistic economy, the form of community is also changing. Relationship is counted based on reciprocity. Philosophically, the community interpreted based on communion. It is not a communion of equals (of same species) but with the whole cosmos. Our very being exists in relation to other beings. Anthropological studies reveal that community is based on commonality, consciousness and commercial values. Commonality is understood, in terms of interest, locality and social system. Consciousness may mean the world of meanings in the minds of the people i.e. symbols, sign etc. Commercial invokes the aspect of community that survives on the mutual benefits received whether it may be of material or spiritual. Religious tradition understands community in terms of communication with fellow beings as well as with the divine. It is only in right communication and relation with the divine that we can relate with others. Biblical tradition offers to say that community is a family where each individual life is affirmed and receives identity. It is a community of friendship and fellowship that brings people together from different backgrounds to participate in building a new community caricatured by love, justice and service. Also, Church is a kind of community which is characterized by friendship and fellowship, which is guided the spirit of mutuality and sharing. Therefore, community is not just a reality to be understood rather it is the very essence of life which provides meaning for one's existence and Church as a community stand as a platform to render this service to its people. In the succeeding chapter, it is intended to look in detail the Moltmann interpretation of community and understand how it would explain convincingly the role and function of the Church as a community in the world.

## Endnotes

[1] Jurgen Moltmann, *The Way of Jesus Christ: Christology in Messianic Dimension* (London: SCM Press, 1990), 268.

[2] Radhakamal Mukherjee, *The Community of Communities* (Bombay: Manaktalas, 1966), 22; cited by Mathew Varghese, *An Appraisal of the Concept of Community in the Writings of Leonardo Boff and Select Indian Christian Theologians to Develop a Theology of the Community' in the Indian Context,* A Dissertation Submitted to the Senate of Serampore College for the Degree of Doctor of Theology, 2004., 15. Also refer Donald E. Hall, *Subjectivity* (New York: Routledge, 1960).

[3] Ibid., 269.

[4] J. Messner, "Community" in *The New Catholic Encyclopedia*, Vol. 4 (New York: McGraw-Hill Book Company, 1967), 81.

[5] Lionel Caplan, "From 'Community' to 'communities' in the Indian Church? in Culture, Religion and Society: Essays in honour of Richard W. Taylor, edited by S.K. Chaterjee and H.P. Mabry (Delhi: ISPCK, 1996), 91.

[6] Mircea Eliade ed., *The Encyclopedia of Religion*, 12 (New York: Macmillan, 1989), 302.

[7] Gunter Remmling and Robert B. Campbell, *Basic Sociology: An Introduction to the Study of Society* (New Jersey: Littlefield Adams, 1976), 214.

[8] Quoted by H.K. Rawat, *Sociology: Basic Concepts* (New Delhi: Rawat Publications, 2007), 64-65.

[9] R.M. McIver and C.H. Page, *Society- An Introductory Analysis,* 1950, 9; cited by G.R. Madan, *Theoretical Sociology* (New Delhi: Mittal publications, 1991), 358.

[10] Leo. F. Schnore, *"Community" in Sociology: An Introduction,* edited by Neil J. Smelser (New Delhi: Wiley Eastern, 1970), 46.

[11] Varghese, *An Appraisal of the Concept of Community in the Writings of Leonardo Boff and Select Indian Christian Theologians to Develop a Theology of the Community' in the Indian Context,* 14.

[12] Messner, *The New Catholic Encyclopedia,* 80.

[13] Ibid.

[14] Ibid., 81.

[15] Ibid.

[16] Ibid.

[17] Walter Kasper, *Theology and Church* (New York: Crossroads, 1989), 148.

[18] Nicholas Sagorsky, *Ecumenism, Christian Origins and the Practice of Communion* (Cambridge: University Press, 2000), 81.

[19] Refer John Rawls, *The Theory of Justice* (London, England: Harvard University Press, 1971), 212.

[20] Gunter W. Remmling and Robert B. Campbell, *Basic Sociology: An Introduction to the Study of Society* (New Jersey: Littlefield Adam, 1976), 215-217.

[21] Ibid., 215.

[22] Ibid., 216.

[23] Ibid.

[24] Ibid., 217.

[25] Salvador Giner, *Sociology* (London: Martin Robertson, 1972), 112.

[26] David L. Sills ed., *International Encyclopedia of the Social Sciences,* Vol. 3 (London: Macmillan, 1972), 172.

[27] Giner, *Sociology...,*113.

[28] Johannes A. Van Der Ven, *Ecclesiology in Context* (Grand Rapids: William E.B. Eerdmans, 1993), 236.

[29] Donald Light et.al., *Reading and Review for Sociology* (New York: McGraw-Hill, 1989), 194.

[30] Bastiaan Wielengen, "With Nagas found in Different Society" in *Christian Witness in Society*, edited by K.C. Abraham (Bangalore: BTESSC, 1998), 147-148.

[31] B. Anderson, *Imagined Communities: Reflections on the Origin and Spread of Nationalism* (London: Verso, 1983) cited by Lionel Caplan, "From 'Community' to 'Communities' in the Indian Church? in *Culture, Religion and Society: Essays in Honour of Richard W. Taylor*, edited by S.K. Chaterjee and H.P. Mabry (Delhi: ISPCK, 1996), 92.

[32] Refer F. Leron Shults, *Reforming Theological Anthropology: After the Philosophical Turn to Relationality* (Michigan: W.B. Eerdmans, 2003).

[33] Mukherjee, *The Community of Communities*, 6.

[34] Ibid., 29.

[35] Mukherjee, Op.cit., 21.

[36] Aristotle, *Metaphysics* bilingual edition, translated by Hugh Tredennick (Cambridge: Harvard University Press, 1933), 292-295.

[37] Vitor Westhelle, *The Church Event: Call and Challenge of a Church Protestant* (Minneapolis: Fortress Press, 2010), 32-33.

[38] Robert Redfield, *The Little Community and Peasant Society and Culture* (Chicago: University of Chicago Press, 1960), 4.

[39] Nigel Rapport and Joanna Overing, *Key Concepts in Social and Cultural Anthropology* (New York: Routledge, 2004), 61.

[40] Anthony Cohen, *The Symbolic Construction of Community* (Chichester: Harwood, 1985), 98.

[41] John B. Chettimattam, *Patterns of Indian Thought* (Mary knoll: Orbis, 1971), 26.

[42] M. Yamunacharya, *Ramanuja's Teachings in his own Words* (Bombay: Bharatiya Vidya Bhavan, 1970), 26.

[43] Cyriac Kanichai, "Satsang vis-à-vis Community Life" in *Third Millennium* 3/4 (April 2000): 122-128.

[44] Chettimattam, *Patterns...*, 40.

[45] "Sangha and Society," in *The Encyclopedia of Religion*, Vol. 13, edited by Miercea Eliade (New York: MacMillan, 1987).

[46] Ibid.

[47] "Religion, Community and Society" in *The Encyclopedia of Religions*, 1987.

[48] Peter Harvey, *An Introduction to Buddhism: Teachings, History and Practices* (Cambridge: University Press, 1997), 73.

[49] Ibid., 236.

[50] V.S. Lalrinawma, *Major Faith Traditions of India* (Delhi: ISPCK, 2007), 253.

[51] William Darrow, "Ummah" in *The Encyclopedia of Religions*, edited by Mircea Eliade (New York: MacMillan Publishing Company, 1987), 123.

[52] "Ummah" *The Oxford Encyclopedia of the Modern Islamic World* Vol. 4, edited by John L. Esposito (New York: Oxford University, 1995), 266.

[53] Mahmoud Ayoub, *Islam: Faith and History* (England: One World Publications, 2006), 43.

[54] M. Hasan, "Indian Iftaar Parties: is it more politics than fellowship" in *The Hindu* Newspaper, September 19, 2010.

[55] Yanghkahao Vashum, "Towards a Tribal Theology of Eco-Human Rights: Resources from the Tangkhul Tradition," in *Journal of Tribal Studies* Vol. 3 No.1 (January-June 1999): 50.

[56] Panger Imchen, *Ancient Ao Naga Religion and Culture* (Delhi: Har-Anand, 1993), 22.

[57] The creation story speaks the fact of God having communion with his creation. But human choice has disrupted this community and as a result God took initiative for redemption and intervenes in human history.

[58] Julio R. Sabanes, "Biblical Understanding of Community," in *Man in Community: Christian Concern for the Human in Changing Society*, edited by Egbert De Vries (New York: Association, 1966), 168.

[59] In OT, there are ample evidences which support the importance of community life in accordance with the will of God. Their understanding of God starts from the belief in God who is the creator, and in whose image, human is made, and who is ever at work in the history.

[60] T. Ralph Morton, *Community of Faith* (New York: Association Press, 1954), 27.

[61] H.P. Muller, "Qahal," *Theological Lexicon of the Old Testament*, edited by Ernst Jenni and Claus Westermann, translated by Mark E. Biddle (Massachusetts: Hendrickson, 1997), 3:1119.

[62] That is, an assembly of Jewish cultic community by the King or the post-exilic leadership for religious purpose in epochal moments in the

history of salvation (1 Chro 28:8; 29:1, 10, 20; 2 Chro 29:28, 31f; 30:2, 4; Ezra 10:12, 14; Nehe 8:2, 17; 13:1).

[63] It has got varied connotations. 1. Deut 33:5 and 1 Chro 12:18 denotes a political entity, a pre-constitution confederation. 2. It implies association (Deut 22:10) with cosmic implication (Is 11:6f). In a military context, it means 'to be together against someone' (Is 9:20), encamping together (Josh 9:2; 11:2). 3. In the Forensic sense, it implies the equality before law and identity of punishment (Is 43:9; 50:8; Jer 6:11, 21). 4. In everyday life people live together, meet together, build house together etc (Gen 13:6; 22:6,8; Deut 25:5; Jud 19:6; Ezra 4:3 etc). 5. In the Prophetic notion of reunited Kingdom, it refers to the new community of the people of God (Ps 102:2, 3; Jer 3:18 etc). H. Fabry, "Yahad" in *Theological Dictionary of the Old Testament*, edited by G. Johannes Botterweck and Helmer Riggen, translated by David E. Green (Grand Rapids, Michigan: W.M.B. Eerdmans, 1990), 6:40.

[64] Bernard W. Anderson, *Contours of Old Testament Theology* (Minneapolis: Fortress Press, 1999), 33.

[65] Herbert Livingston, *The Pentateuch in its Cultural Environment* (Grand Rapids,: Baker,1987), 162.

[66] Elmer A. Martens, *God's Design: A Focus on Old Testament Theology* (Grand Rapids, Michigan: Baker, 1987), 66.

[67] Sigmund Mowinkel, *The Psalms in Israel's Worship* (New York: Abingdon Press, 1962), 42.

[68] Terence Fretheim, *The Pentateuch* (Nashville: Abingdon Press, 1996), 47-48.

[69] Ibid., 18.

[70] John P. Meier, *A Marginal Jew: Rethinking the Historical Jesus* (New York: Doubleday, 2001), 232.

[71] Donald Guthrie, *The New Testament Theology* (London: IVP, 1981), 706.

[72] Robert W. Wall, "Community," in *Anchor Bible Dictionary* Vol.1, edited by David Noel Freedman (New York: Doubleday, 1992), 1:1105.

[73] Sozanne De Deitrich, *The Witnessing Community* (Philadelphia: Westminster Press, 1958), 132.

[74] J.A.T. Robinson, *The Body: A Study in Pauline Theology* (London: SCM Press, 1963), 27.

[75] Paul D. Hanson, *The People Called: The Growth of Community in the Bible* (San Francisco: Harper and Row, 1985), 442.

[76] Varghese, *An Appraisal of the Concept of Community in the Writings of Leonardo Boff and Select Indian Christian Theologians to Develop a Theology of the Community' in the Indian Context*, 92.

[77] Hanson, *The People Called*, 470.

[78] Robert W. Wall, "Community" in *Anchor Bible Dictionary*, edited by David Noel Freedman, Vol.1 (New York: Doubleday, 1992), 1108.

[79] John D. Zizioulas, *Being as Communion: Studies in Personhood and Church* (New York: St. Vladimir Seminary, 1985), 18. also refer Veli Matti Karkainnen, Veli-Matti Karkkainen, *An Introduction to Ecclesiology* (Illinois: Intervarsity Press, 2002), 95-102.

[80] Miroslav Volf, *The Church as the Image of the Trinity* (Grand Rapids: Eerdmans Publishing Company, 1998), 101.

[81] Wolfhart Pannenberg, *Systematic Theology*, vol. 3 (Grand Rapids: Eerdmans, 1998), 463-470.

[82] Dietrich Bonhoeffer, *No Rusty Swords* (New York: Harper and Row, 1965), 112-113.

[83] John B. Cobb, Jr. and David Ray Griffin, *Process Theology: An Introductory Exposition* (Belfast, Ireland: Westminster Press, 1976), 114-115.

---
## CHAPTER- 2
# Church as Community: Ecclesiology of Jurgen Moltmann

## Introduction

The previous chapter has provided substantial accounts on community from various perspectives. As community has been indispensable part of human existence, Moltmann too has pondered on this aspect to understand the mystery of the church. Therefore, this chapter would look into the background of Moltmann's theological enterprise and would focus on questions like How Moltmann is unique and different in his understanding of community from other discussed perspectives? How the concept of community is used to elaborate Moltmann ecclesiological interest?

## The Life and Context of Jurgen Moltmann

Jurgen Moltmann was born in Hamburg, Germany, on April 8, 1926.[1] The name 'Moltmann' means 'the man' of a farmer 'Molt' belonging to the parchim region and is of Slavic origin.[2] He was brought up in a real community marked by shared festivities, sports group and neighbourly help. His father was an authority in German, Latin and History. He pledged to a life of 'plain living and high thinking' which he received from his father Johannes Moltmann, a free thinker who lived in the optimistic spirit of the opening years of the German empire.[3] His father joined the 'League of German Ramblers' and volunteered for the army. His mother, who came from Schwerin, was a kind lady and had a cheerful and happy nature. She was brought up in a rich family with her father being the director of archives. He was raised in an enlightened liberal Protestant home. This liberal environment provided a rightful platform to be fascinated by the writings of poets and philosophers of German Idealism like Lessing, Goethe and Nietzsche than of the Bible. Being born in this tradition, he was deficient in religious education. He was admitted to pastor Hansen Petersen in 1940 for confirmation classes which did not made any impression on him and left the Lutheran church. In Gottingen, he joined the Reformed congregation for the gospel's sake,[4] which became the substrate for his calling.

Like all German men, he fought in World War II. At the age of 14, Moltmann joined the Hitler youth camp. Appalled by the situation in the camp and its training, he got conviction that he was not born to be one of a mass, and his determination to be alone rather than to be ordered about. In 1943, his desire to be trained in the Nazi camp was over and was replaced by the military lunacy.[5] In February 1943, his school class was enrolled for the air force auxiliaries and was stationed with the Alster anti-aircraft battery in Shwanenwieck. In July 24, 1943, one of the most dreadful 'Operation Gomorrah' was launched by the British for the complete destruction of the first big German city. In this war the English raided the German cities with air bombers. The Bombing left many places totally destroyed raising the death toll to 40,000 in that period. During one of the nights for the first time Moltmann remembered God and cried out to him and surrendered himself. He says, "I was as if dead, and ever after received life every day as a new gift. My question was not, 'Why does God allow this to happen? But, 'My God, where are you?' And there was the other question: why am I alive and not dead, too, like the friend at my side? I felt the guilt of survival and searched for the meaning of continued life. I knew that there had to be some reason why I was still alive. During that night I became a seeker after God."[6] Moltmann was held as prisoner of war during this period. Moltmann received his doctoral degree in theology in 1952 and served as pastor of a small Reformed Church in Wasserhorst until 1957. Later he became a teacher of theology at the academy operated by the confessing Church at Wuppertal. After a brief period at the University of Bonn, Moltmann was offered the prestigious position of professor of systematic theology at the University of Tübingen and accepted the visiting professorship in the United States.[7]

## Foundations for Jurgen Moltmann's Theological Writings

## The Prison Experience

As Moltmann was involved in the World War II, he was captured by the British in Belgium in 1945 and held as a prisoner of war until 1948. As the Prisoner of war, he received some unexpected hospitality from the British counterparts. Moltmann along with 200 more prisoners were put inside a barbed wire fence. They were helped to remove their unhygienic appearance and provided new dresses with numbers on it. The primary source for his theology came from the experience of camp in Belgium, Scotland and England. The experience in the camps brought a crisis of faith in Moltmann's life. He writes, "In the camps in Belgium and Scotland I experienced both the collapse of those things that had been certainties for me and a new hope to live by, provided by the Christian faith. I probably owe to this hope, not only my mental and moral but physical survival as well, for it was what saved me from despairing and giving up. I came back a Christian, with a new "personal goal" of studying theology, so that I might understand the power of hope to which I owed my life."[8] This brought a religious conversion and opened his eyes to God who is with the brokenhearted. He found that God was still present in his condition. He says, "All that was left was an inward drive, a longing which provided the impetus to hope."[9] In the summer of 1947, an international SCM conference after the war, held in Swanwick, completely turned his life around. It was a place made for the sharing of war experiences. In that event, they were welcomed as brothers in Christ and ate and drink, prayed and sang together with young Christians, who had come from Australia and New Zealand. This experience provided a platform for reconciliation that brought a sense of liberation and breathed air of new courage. It became an unfading mark on the life of Moltmann which prompted him to pursue theological training and understand from the perspective of suffering and hope in God that constitutes two sides of the same coin.

## Influences of Theologians and Philosophers

Moltmann, in his early years, studied theology under the
teachers who were strongly influenced by Karl Barth. As a
result, he too passionately became an ardent admirer and
follower of Barth, which did not last long. Soon he became
critical of Barth's theology as it neglected the historical nature
of reality and the eschatological nature of theology.[10] The chaos
and destruction witnessed by Moltmann in the post-World war
II awakened him for the quest of understanding the role of
the Church in the society. To achieve this quest, as Baukham
says, Moltmann engaged himself in a serious study of
Bonhoeffer's work, from which, as well as from Ernst Wolf, he
developed his concern for social ethics and the Church's
involvement in the secular society.[11] Moltmann was convinced
of the liberating truth of the Reformation doctrine of
justification and theology of the cross of Luther. The influence
of Hegel and Hans Joachim Iwand contributed to the
development of his dialectical interpretation of the cross and
the resurrection.[12] He studied Biblical theology from Gerhard
von Rad and Ernst Kasemann. Otto Weber, who supervised
his doctorates and his future wife- Elizabeth Wendel, helped
him gain the eschatological perspective of the Church's
universal mission toward the coming kingdom of God.
Continual discussion with her opened his eyes to many things
which he should "probably otherwise have overlooked;" it also
made him conscious of the "psychological and social limitation"
of his "male point of view and judgement."[13]Another catalyst
that molded theological conviction of Moltmann came from
the work of Jewish Marxist philosopher Ernst Bloch in 1959.
He envisaged his 'Theology of Hope' as a kind of theological

parallel to Bloch's 'Philosophy of Hope,' which kept him in dialogue with Bloch throughout his theological career. He admits that it was Bloch who helped him to see the Marxist inheritance of Jewish messianism, which subsequently became a major influence in his writings and ministry.[14] In the early 1970s, he took up important concepts from the critical theory of the Frankfurt School. The influence of Jewish theologians such as Franz Rosenzweig and Abraham Heschel can be found at many points in his work.[15]

## A Survey on Moltmann's Theological Enterprise

Moltmann's theological enterprise is clubbed into two distinct series. The first series is the trilogy that comprises of *Theology of Hope-* which tries to see the eschatological orientation of the whole of theology, *The Crucified God-* which is an attempt to view crucified Christ as the criterion of Christian theology, and *The Church in the Power of the Holy Spirit-* which complements these two angles of approach with an ecclesiological and pneumatological perspective. The most important controlling theological idea in Moltmann's early work is his dialectical interpretation of the Cross and the Resurrection of Jesus, which is then subsumed into the particular form of trinitarianism which becomes the over-arching principle of his later work. 'Theology of Hope' presents the resurrection and 'The Crucified God' portrays the cross and the Spirit, whose mission derives from the event of both Cross and Resurrection, bridging a platform between God and the world in 'Church in the Power of the Holy Spirit.'[16] Therefore, these three books stand as a single unitary vision with complementary perspectives.

In the Second series of major works Moltmann aims to present a series of systematic contribution to theology by considering the context and correlations of important concepts and doctrines of Christian theology in a particular systematic sequence. *The Trinity and the Kingdom of God* presents the doctrine of God. *God in Creation* presents the doctrine of creation. *The Way of Jesus Christ* presents Christology. *The Spirit of Life* presents doctrine of Pneumatology. *The Coming of God* presents doctrine of Eschatology. Apart from above series he has written numerous theological books and articles.[17] His most recent work is, *In the Beginning, the End,* published in 2002.

Moltmann was not just involved in writings but his theological procession also included other practical aspects. Apart from his writing, lecturing and teaching, Moltmann has been involved in ecumenical dialogues with Catholics, Orthodox Christians and Jews. In 1960s he was involved in the Christian-Marxist dialogue and tried to build a connection between Christians and revisionist Marxist. His critical engagement with liberation theologians of all kinds has made him a major influence in revolutionary and political theologies of the latter half of the century around the world.

## Theological Method of Jurgen Moltmann

In his early works *Theology of Hope* and *Crucified God*, Moltmann was praxis oriented. He along with the Catholic theologian Johann Baptist Metz was behind the political theology movement during 1960s. It was an attempt to meet the challenges of modernity, characterized by industrialization, urbanization, science and technology and market economy with their common belief in progress and in politics as a means for consciously forming the future.[18] In *Theology of Hope*, he emphasized a strong practical thrust in terms of the mission of the Church to transform the world in anticipation of its promised eschatological transformation by God. However, in his later books there is a shift in his methodology due to its limitations. In his book, *Theology and Joy*, Moltmann became dissatisfied with seeing theology purely as a theory of practice and began to inject elements of contemplation, celebration and doxology in his work. Another reason for the change is that he could not defend his extensive elaboration of the doctrine of Trinity in purely practical terms. Moltmann writes, "Faith lives in meditation and prayer as well as in practice. Without the *vita contemplativa* the *vita activa* quickly becomes debased into activism, falling a victim to the pragmatism of the modern meritocratic society which judges by performance."[19] Third reason for the change in methodology is the present ecological crisis. He thinks it is an essential again to take up "the pre-modern concept of reason as the organ to perception and participation."[20]

Theology of Moltmann is characterized by its openness to dialogue. He is not creating a theological system as a finished task of a theologian and keeps it open for dialogue and inputs.[21] Baukham points out that genuine openness ensures, "that theology does not know all the answers but can learn from other approach to reality."[22]

## 'Community' in the writings of Jurgen Moltmann

One of the major topics that Moltmann give attention is the nature of community in the life and teachings of the Church.

He has provided some significant contribution in the area of ecclesial enterprise by unfolding rainbows of reflection from the community concept. His enumeration of community understanding can be highlighted in his work *History and the Triune God, Trinity and the Kingdom of God, Church in the Power of the Holy Spirit and The Open Church*. This section would try to bring about those salient features that cover his community concept.

## Church as Community

The underlying mark of any Church, for Moltmann, is 'one, holy, catholic and apostolic Church. Unity in freedom, holiness in poverty, catholicity in partisan support for the weak, and apostolate in suffering constitute this mark.[23] Moltmann believes that Church is not just about believing in Jesus Christ and following the marks of the Church but also a community of brothers and sisters who shares common life in Christ. As he quotes from Barmen Declaration which in turn taken from article VII of Augsburg confession which says, "The Christian Church is the *community of brethren*." A 'community of brethren' lives in the spirit of brotherliness, showing its fellowship with God's son, 'the first-born among many brethren' (Rom 8:29), through a brotherly common life.[24] The act of this community is fellowship not only in terms of coming together to proclaim the gospel, but it goes beyond in celebrating a holistic life that is embraced and shared with one another. As he says, "the assembly of believers…embraces the whole of life, our dealings with one another, our representation for others and our common actions."[25] This holistic life, for Moltmann, is not hidden rather reflected through one's life and activities. If community represents the people belonging to a particular belief, ideas and common goal marked by unity, equality and fraternity then Church is a community because of all these aspects inherent in it. In other words, Church becomes community only in relation to others which is characterized by equality, friendship and fellowship.

## Trinitarian Community: Community of Unity and Equality

The unity of the community is in truth the trinitarian fellowship of God himself, of which it is a reflection and in which it participates. The community is the 'lived out' Trinity.[26] In the community, mutual love is practiced which corresponds to the eternal love of the Trinity. Mirroring the egalitarian relationship between the trinitarian persons, the Church is a communion of equals. It is a critical response to the hierarchical presentation of Trinity by the Church that only demanded authority over the subjects. It is the Holy Spirit that brings the unity in its visible form i.e. the fellowship of brothers and sisters without superiors or inferiors. It is a fellowship of men and women freed through love. He tried to integrate the femininity into the dignity of the image of God where the Holy Spirit is taken as mother along with Father and Son and all other people of the world as community of brothers and sisters, not just of brothers. In order to substantiate the dynamics of this fellowship, Moltmann subscribes the idea of motherhood of Holy Spirit from Zizendorf, who founded the first American community of brothers and sisters in Pennsylvania in 1741. He quotes, "That the Father of our Lord Jesus Christ is our true Father and the Spirit of Jesus Christ is our true Mother; because the Son of the living God, his one, only begotten son, is our true brother… The Father must love us and cannot do otherwise, the Mother must guide us through the world and cannot do otherwise, and the son, our Brother, must love the soul as his own soul, the body as his own body, because we are flesh of his flesh and bone of his bone, and he cannot do otherwise."[27] In its feminine and motherly characteristics the fellowship of the Holy Spirit has a healing, liberating and sensitizing effect. It seems that Moltmann's social doctrine of the Trinity actually is a product of social and political considerations which create a God in the image of a theologian's ideal of an egalitarian society. It also reinforces Feuerbach's thesis that the concept of trinity is nothing more than the projection into the heavens of the idealized human essence.[28]

## Perichoretic Community

The community model of unity and equality receives its purpose from the relationship of Father, Son and the Holy Spirit in terms of *perichoresis* which means 'the exchange of divine energies,' where the Father exists in the Son, the Son in the Father, and both of them in the Spirit, just as the Spirit exists in both the Father and Son…. the Father, the Son and the Spirit dwell in one another and communicate life to one another.[29] As the Father, the Son and the Spirit communicate life to one life so also God shares his life with the world. It is a relationship of fellowship, mutual need and mutual interpenetration.[30] Therefore he conceived his community as a fellowship of liberated nature, humans and God existing in harmony on an equal footing, instead of the monarchy of the glorious Lord of creation over all. For him God does not dominate the world claiming everything as its creation at his disposal rather he involves himself to affect and be affected from his creation. He says, "On the Sabbath the resting God begins to "experience" the beings he has created. The God who rests in the face of his creation does not dominate the world on this day; he "feels" the world; he allows himself to be affected, to be touched by each of his creatures. He adopts the community of creation as his own milieu."[31] Philosophically it is cosmic in nature but theologically it is a *Theocosmic* community. God's goal for the persons is not that they be his servants or children but his friends, and "in friendship the distance enjoined by sovereignty ceases to exist."[32] It means that only in friendship that a Perichoretic community can exist in unity and equality. It is important, therefore, that the Christian culture should rediscover the biblical concept of God's tri-unity as community and fellowship among three equal persons, not a monarchy of one person over the others and the world.

## Community of Friendship and fellowship

The visible expression of the egalitarian community can be expressed in terms of friendship which is not a teleological bond rather affective bond. He uses the term 'friend' instead of 'brother' because the former connotes the presence of freedom, but the latter demands love and allegiance. The friend is a person 'who loves in freedom' without any goal motivation. Friendship is a free association, a new relationship, which goes beyond the social roles of those involved. It is an open relationship which spreads friendliness, because it combines affection with respect. This open friendship prepares the ground for a friendlier world.[33] The community of brethren, is really the fellowship of friends who live in the friendship of Jesus and spread friendliness in the fellowship, by meeting the forsaken with affection and the despised with respect.[34] The life in the friendship of Jesus is rooted in the free giving of his life 'for his friends.'[35] In the friendship, no condition of conflicts or disagreements and quarrels can take space for long even though it might exist superficially because a true friend only gives and not expect to receive. That is why even unfriendliness cannot destroy this friendship of Jesus.

But how are friendship and fellowship realized in the church? What form have they taken and what form can they take? The church grew out of Christ's fellowship. Out of his fellowship it is born anew. The community of the brethren springs from the brotherhood of Christ, and from brotherliness it will acquire a new form. As friends they live from the friendship of Jesus. From the spirit of friendship, they will form themselves anew.[36] The present crisis in the church seems to tantalize believers and undertake the task of reform and renewal. But this situation can only be rectified when the church acts together in practical fellowship. It is only in the friendship and fellowship among each other irrespective of rank and file that church can unveil its dirty nature of individualism and traditionalism that disfigures the true nature of the church.

Where to begin this renewal? Moltmann says that the congregation itself should be the starting point. The fellowship among the people, in word and sacrament, profession of faith, institution and hierarchy becomes lifeless if friendship is not recovered from the 'grass-roots.'[37] The 'grass-roots' community is the primary, fundamental core of the church. On its own level it must take responsibility for the riches of faith and for its propagation, as well as for the cult, which brings faith to expression. It is consequently the initial cell of the church's structure, the focus of evangelization, and at present the main point of departure for man's improvement and development. Moltmann designs the characteristics of this community in the following way. 1. The voluntary association of members in a Christian fellowship. 2. The fellowship of a manageable size, in which life is mutual friendship and common devotion to a specific task, is possible. 3. The awakening of creative powers in every individual and the surrender of privileges that members bring with them. 4. Autonomy in forming the spiritual life of the community and its life of fellowship. 5. Common concentration on special Christian tasks in society, whether be it in the field of evangelization, or the liberation of the under-privileged and oppressed. 6. The deliberate return to a simple Christo-centrism in the devotional life and to a reflection of new Christian practice in theology.[38]

## Church as Messianic Community

If the Trinitarian community realizes the unity and equality through friendship and fellowship, then it has got messianic character. "The messianic community belongs to the Messiah and the messianic word; and this community, with the powers that it has, already realizes the possibilities of the messianic era which brings the gospel of the kingdom to the poor, which proclaims the lifting of the downtrodden to the lowly, and begins the glorification of the coming God through the actions of hope in the fellowship of the poor, and the sad and those condemned to silence, so that it may lay hold on all men."[39] Therefore his community must be a messianic fellowship oriented in mission towards the coming kingdom of God. Thus, church does not exist for itself but in the service of the kingdom of God in the world. The messianic fellowship is therefore, the fellowship of those who participate in the mission of Christ.

This eschatological mission of Christ is not only Christological but also cater the pneumatological perspective. It's fellowship with Christ is founded on the experience of the Spirit which manifests Christ, unites us with him and glorifies him in humans. Its fellowship in the kingdom of God is founded on the power of the Spirit, which leads it into truth and freedom. It is when the church, out of faith in Christ and in hope for the kingdom, sees itself as the messianic fellowship then it will logically understand its presence and its path in the presence and process of the Holy Spirit.[40] The church in the power of the Spirit is not yet the kingdom of God, but it is its anticipation in history. The way from the history of Christ to his future is also the history of the Spirit in his work of unification and glorification through which the eschatological future enters history.[41] In other words, the Spirit takes into itself the history of Christ and enters into the eschatological future. Therefore, messianic fellowship witnesses the church that not only engages visibly in the world but also moves around with a messianic mission in history and augments its anticipation towards the eschatological fulfillment in the power and presence of the Spirit.

## Sacramental Community

What are the criteria for being a part of the messianic community? Moltmann says that it is through Sacraments that one enters into the messianic community. Baptism and Lord's Supper belong essentially together and are linked with one another in the messianic community. In the Baptismal event the community is linked to the individual who enters the fellowship of Christ and confesses publicly. Joining in a community through baptism is a liberating event which in turn spreads the liberty of Christ to our fellow brethren.[42] Moltmann cautions that baptism should not become the symbol of inner emigration and resignation in the face of the wicked world rather it should be a sign of the dawn of hope for this world. In eating and drinking at the Lord's Table individuals are linked to the community which is visible in these acts. Baptism and the Lord's Supper are the signs of the church's life, because they are the signs of the one who is their life. They are in this way the public signs of the church's confession of faith because they show the one who leads the world into the liberty of the divine life. If entering into the messianic community requires baptism and Lord's Supper, then how about those outside of the Christian fold? In a multi-religious context, it again presupposes for a closed community alien to the needs of the world. Moltmann's concept of the church as a community of open friendship strongly influences his proposals on the meaning and practice of the Lord's Supper.[43] It confers the fellowship which derives from Christ's self-giving on the cross and so 'creates solidarity among people who are in themselves are different.'[44] The fellowship round the Lord's Table must be in principle open to the whole world, since it is based on Jesus' table-fellowship not only with his disciples but also with the poor and unrighteous. Since, it derives from the crucified Christ's open identification with all the godless and the godforsaken. It also points in anticipation to the eschatological banquet of the nations. The only condition which can be set for participation in the supper is 'that we be clear that in this meal we have to do with the Jesus who is crucified for us and that in this meal the kingdom of God stands open to us.'[45] Moltmann explains further about the open community through the concept of Open Church.

## The Open Church

Moltmann finds the messianic fellowship as relational, as he depicts in the trinitarian history of God. He says just the Father, Son and Spirit work for the unification and glorification of all things in triune God, in the same way church, which is not just a mediator but also, exists in relationship with others. The movement which is found in the trinitarian mission also includes the church that moves along with the partners in history, engage with them, open to change, and direct these relationships in hope towards the common future of the Kingdom of God. To put it differently in the words of Baukham, church fulfills its messianic vocation not by absolutizing itself but in open relationship of dialogue and co-operation.[46] Because of the church relative place in the wider context of the trinitarian history of God, it is "open for God, open for men and open for the future of both God and men. The Church atrophies when it surrenders any one of this openness and closes itself up against God, humanity or the future."[47] Here Moltmann is taking a different stance from anthropological notion that stress on commonality in interest and locality. He attests that Church as a community should neither based on commonality nor communality rather in open relation to other those who are different.

How church can live for the world? Moltmann says that it is through participating in the offices (Prophetic, Priestly and Kingly) of Christ. The church participates in all of these in its response to God's invitation to be an instrument of salvation. In other words, church participates in liberating the people in bondage, solidarity with weak and helpless, fellowship of freedom and equality in the Spirit.[48] Church does not live for itself but rather exists for others. Therefore, the church lives for and out of mission. But even the mission has to be shaped by the principle of openness. "Israel, the world religions, and the economic and political, and cultural processes of the world" are partners in history "who are not the church and will never become the church."[49] To put it differently, the mission of the church is not to 'spread the church but to spread the kingdom.' The church is not self-serving but serving the world and the kingdom.[50] Thus church acts as a substrate in the preparation of a kingdom where all are invited. This invitation, according to Moltmann, is based on love and can be experienced and represented only in the comprehensible congregation in which one sees and recognizes the other and accepts the other as he or she is accepted in Christ.[51] Therefore the urgent task of Christianity is to recover the congregational nature of the Church. As he says, "there is in the church nothing higher than the congregation."[52] But today it is observed that the Church is moving its relationship on a contractual basis i.e. profit based relationship. The community which was based on natural will of interdependence is taking a new shape of community based on rational will for individual ends.

## Community of the Cross

What is that dynamic act which threads the community in love, friendship and fellowship at the same time open itself to the world? It is under the cross of Christ that the church as a community becomes the instrument of love, justice and friendship. Moltmann provides three historical reasons for the death of Christ on the cross and its significance for the community later. Firstly, the godlessness of Jesus, which he brought through his engagement with the religious leaders and the laws of his day that ended in his death, secured the righteousness of the outcaste, and justice for those without rights. In other words, Jesus act on the cross brought liberation from the compulsion of sin and is no longer a sinner anymore. Through the Christ's surrender of himself to death on the cross brought about forgiveness of sin by his blood to a new life and new righteousness. Moltmann quoting Luther says that on the cross a 'merry exchange' took place in which Christ and the soul become one body, Christ makes the soul's sin and suffering his own, conferring on him in his poverty his own righteousness, his freedom and his divinity.[53] In other words, the suffering of humans became the history of Christ and the freedom of Christ became the history of humans. Anyone who lives in the righteousness of Christ through the experience of the forgiveness of sins is 'dead' to the legal systems of life in this world. He no longer accepts the inescapability of that law and its consequences. The new life of community under the cross will never succumb to the evil systems of the world and will stand for the cause of new creation where justice, love and friendship prevail.

Secondly, the cross not only brought liberation from the law but also from the power of the world. Jesus preaching of the kingdom of God became a snare to the political kingdom of Romans which was culminated in the death of Christ on the cross. In so far as the community of Christ as a whole is born 'from the wound in Christ's side,' it will also as whole, through its existence and way of life, be a fervent to break down political idolatry.[54] It will press for the desacralization of political power and the democratization of the political rule. Also, Jesus' torture, mocking, rejection and crucifixion 'outside the gate' (Heb 13:12), he enters the company of the despised, tortured, the rejected and the murdered. His public execution together with two robbers is the sign of his solidarity with these lost people. He was bringing the liberating rule of God into the situation of deepest abandonment. In other words, as the community of crucified Jesus the church is drawn into his self-surrender, into his solidarity with the lost, and into his public suffering. His suffering is in this respect not exclusive but inclusive and leads to compassion.

Thirdly, Jesus died on the cross not merely as a condemned blasphemer and as an executed rebel, but also as one forsaken by God. In his abandonment by God the son of God takes upon himself both the fate of man who has been forsaken by God. Through Jesus' experience of the Godforsakenness, he is bringing those who are forsaken to the eternal love of God. In the Son's cross God takes this death on himself in order to give those who are lost his own eternal life. In other words, as Jesus, being abandoned brings those forsaken to God, in the same way God who experience pain in giving of his son to death comes closer to those who are away from God. In this happening God is revealed as the trinitarian God, and in the event between the surrendering Father and the forsaken son, God becomes so 'vast' in the Spirit of self-offering that there is room and life for the whole world, the living and the dead.[55] Thus, the community of Christ experiences fellowship only in the light of the Cross. This fellowship in the community is experienced in common resistance to idolatry and inhumanity, in common suffering over oppression and persecution. It is this participation in the passion of Christ and in the passion of the people that the 'life' of Christ and his liberty becomes visible in the Church. In short, the community formed by the cross is not complementary to the religiously moral community rather a community that is based on self-giving.

## Community in the Process of the Spirit

If the community cherishes its dynamic nature under the cross of Christ, then the Holy Spirit makes it functional in the lives of the believers today. The purpose of the community is to establish peace and freedom in the chaotic world and it is the through the gifts and powers of the liberating Spirit in the community that directs towards the world freed from the 'elemental spirits.' Pneumatological dimension to ecclesiology makes possible the fullest description of the life of the church. He writes, "It is the doctrine of the Holy Spirit in particular that depicts the processes and experiences in which and through which the church becomes comprehensible to itself as the

messianic fellowship in the world for the world."[56] As Church
is the creation of the Spirit, it is a charismatic fellowship of
equal persons. That is why there is neither Jew nor Greek,
there is neither slave nor free, there is neither male nor female;
for you all are one in Christ (Gal 3:28). In Christ a person
appears as God's person, not as Greek, a Scythian, a slave or
a freeman. Though God has chosen certain people for the
ministry like apostles, teaches, prophets etc., their commission
does not separate them from the people and does not set them
above people either, for it is exercised in fellowship with and
by commission of the whole people and in the name of that
people's commissioning. The Spirit calls them into life; the
Spirit gives the community the authority for its mission. The
ministry of the Church is charismatic in essence. Moltmann
points out that the ministry is turned into an "insipid, spiritless,
kind of civil service and charisma becomes a cult of the
religious genius, if we do not make the one charismatically
living community our point of departure."[57]

Moltmann wants to emphasize the role of charismata in
the church, but he does so by expanding the often too narrow
understanding of spiritual gifts. According to Moltmann, "when
a person is called, whatever he is and brings with him becomes
a charismata through his calling, since he is accepted by the
Spirit and put at the service of the Kingdom of God."[58] Thus
a gentile brings his gentile existence into the community. Being
a woman is a charisma and must not be surrendered in favour
of patriarchal and male ways of thinking and behaving."[59] The
Holy Spirit gives spiritual gifts for the service of the world, for
example, prophetic speech in liberation and in the ecological

movements. The charismata are by no means to be seen merely in the 'special ministries' of the gathered community. Every member of the messianic community is a charismatic, not only in the community's solemn assemblies but every day, when members are scattered and isolated in the world. He writes, "... everything a person is, and everything that has molded that person become a charisma, if he or she is called by Christ, and loves life, and helps to work for the Kingdom of God."[60]

The work of the Spirit is not confined to the church because the spirit works everywhere in creation. In his words, it is the *community of creation* that recognizes the operation of the life-giving Spirit of God in the trend to relationship in created things.[61] Therefore, the church cannot absolutize itself, but it is always provisional in nature to minister as steward to the world around us. The characteristic and inventive features of the pneumatological ecclesiology of Moltmann are his ecological concern and the challenge to patriarchy. Moltmann clarifies, "there is not only an economy of salvation in the Spirit of God; there is an ecology of salvation."[62] He opposes the traditional limited Pneumatology in the Roman Catholic and Protestant traditions that view Holy Spirit solely as the spirit of redemption and its place in the church is to give assurance of the eternal blessedness of the souls. This makes people turn away from this world and hope for a better world beyond. Moltmann criticizes that theology has been content with talking about Holy Spirit in connection with God, faith, Christian life, the Church and prayer, but seldom in connection with the body and nature. It takes the form of a kind of hostility to the body, a kind of remoteness from the world, and a preference for the inner experiences of the soul rather than the sensory experience of sociality and nature. [63] This limited view of the spirit has impoverished and emptied the churches while the "Spirit emigrates to spontaneous groups and personal experiences."[64] This led him to work out a holistic Pneumatology.

Moltmann criticizes the Protestant theology, which proceed from the Christocentric concept of the church. In Christocentric concept God is the head of Christ, so Christ is the head of the Church and the man obviously the head of women. This Christocentric interpretation leads logically to the exclusion of women from the ministry or spiritual office. He writes, "Both the hierarchical and the Christocentric notions of the church are clerical, because they transfer conditions in the church to family and social relationship between men and women in their secular society, and are ready to make anti-Christian spirit of the age responsible for the protests which consequently arise."[65] Neither hierarchical nor the Christocentric ecclesiology cheers an experienceable outpouring of the Spirit, and they repress the early Christian experience of Pentecost. Moltmann writes, "Whatever accords with the fulfillment of the Joel promise in church and culture is the operation of the Spirit. Whatever contradicts it is spiritless and deadly."[66] According to Moltmann, "In the Holy Spirit a new messianic community of women and men prophesies with the same gifts and the same rights."[67] Therefore, he wants to "start from the early Christian experience of Pentecost" and "to develop a pneumatological concept of the church: there is one spirit and many gifts."[68] Moltmann's firm conviction is that wherever is passion for life, there the Spirit of God operating- life over against oppression, and justice over against life.[69]

The concept of "Community of the Holy Spirit "has been used in theology to refer to the church. Moltmann radically expands this traditionally notion to encompass the whole "community of creation" from the most elementary particles to atoms to molecules to cells to living organisms to animals to human beings to community of humanity. The creation lives in a complex enriching communal relationship interpenetrated by the Spirit of God. Therefore, Moltmann enumerates the process of the Spirit in terms of its activity beyond the traditional notion of Spirit's activity through the gifts and fruits of the Spirit and develops to a more cosmic and eco-friendly community.

## Community for Democratic Social reconstruction

The Community is not intended to be centered on self-edification rather to be 'a prophetic leaven' for the renewal of the Society. Moltmann finds this 'grass-roots' communities have the potential not only in building the church but also the society at large.[70] The Church should use its resources for the service of these communities not the other way round as usually happens. The nature of these communities is to live in open friendship among the people and avoid any sort of esoteric self-isolation. Moltmann argues, if these grass-root communities really offer people the common opportunity for friendship free of domination, then they will be letting the people to be the subject of their own history in the liberating history of God.[71] In other words, through the friendship of the people the church can bring the danger of esoteric self-isolation, loneliness, helplessness and dependency out of the picture. Once these are swept away then these communities will become the substrate for people to be the subject of their own history in the liberating history of God. This grass-root' communities can provide impulses for a fundamental and democratic social construction.[72] In this the community determines its goals and needs, develop the confidence and the will to do something about them through co-operation. Community work aims to put people in a position where they can shape their fortunes for themselves, through initiatives for self-help, in the local sphere. It is not about a welfare work rather it is the aim of the community to come in consciousness of their own identity and their own strength among the people.[73]

## Conclusion

Moltmann reinterprets the ecclesiology beyond the structures and boundaries of the institutionalized church. He has made use of social scientific notions of community with his own theological garnish that consumes any form of hierarchy, parochialism and individualism. When the first chapter dealt with the meaning of community in terms of common interest, locality, filial bonds etc., the second chapter has tried to go beyond these conventional ideas and brought out the content of community in the framework of friendship and fellowship of the messianic Kingdom. For him, Church is a messianic fellowship of committed disciples. The community is not only about filial bonding in Christ but also covers a sense of friendship without any obligatory references. The importance is given more to the concept of friendship than the lordship in messianic community. Moltmann is going away from the traditional notion of community, particularly, as a religious identity for showing strength and presents a community that is open to all without any reservations. The Church in the Spirit can impart the genuine messianic fellowship and serve the world with commitment and determination. Moltmann is different from modern analysis of community in the sense of treating the entire cosmos in the design of God's activity. In this community the differences do not provide hindrance to the community building but become the platform for celebration. Moltmann's community is dialogical in nature which has much relevance for Indian context. The concept of messianic community and open church does play a vital role in the caste oriented Indian society. The Dalits and Tribals are no longer inferior in the community of Jesus.

## Footnotes

[1] Stanley J. Grenz and Roger E. Olson, *20th Century Theology* (Secunderabad: OM Books, 2004), 173.

[2] Jurgen Moltmann, *A Broad Place: An Autobiography*, trans. by Margaret Kohl (Minneapolis, U.S.A: Fortress Press. 2008), 11.

[3] Ibid., 6.

[4] Moltmann, *A Broad Place*, 14.

[5] Ibid., 13.

[6] Ibid., 17.

[7] Tony Lane, *The Lion Book of Christian Thought* (Tiruvalla: Suvartha Bhavan, 1999), 147.

[8] Jurgen Moltmann, "Autobiographical Note" in A.J.Conyers, *God, Hope and History: Jurgen Moltmann and the Christian Concept of History* (Macon, Ga.: Mercer University Press, 1988), 203-223. Quoted by Stanly Grenz and Roger Olson, *20th Century Theology,* 173.

[9] Jurgen Moltmann, *Experience of God* (Philadelphia: Fortress Press, 1980), 8.

[10] M. Douglas Meeks, *Origins of the Theology of Hope* (Philadelphia: Fortress, 1974), 15-53.

[11] Richard Baukham, *The Theology of Jurgen Moltmann* (Edinburgh: T&T Clark, 1995), 2.

[12] Ibid.

[13] Jurgen Moltmann, *The Way of Jesus Christ: Christology in Messianic Dimension*, trans. Margaret Kohl (San Francisco: Harper and Row, 1990), xvii.

[14] Ibid.

[15] Ibid.

[16] Baukham, *Theology of Jurgen Moltmann*, 4-5.

[17] A detailed bibliography of his work till 1995 can be found in the work of Richard Baukham.

[18] For a detailed discussion of the emergence of political theology and especially the contribution of Moltmann see Arne Rasmusson, *The Church as Polis: From Political Theology to Theological Politics as Exemplified by Jurgen Moltmann and Stanley Hauerwas* (Lund: Lund University Press, 1994).

[19] Jurgen Moltmann, *Trinity and the Kingdom of God* (New York: Harper Collins, 1981), 2.

[20] Jurgen Moltmann, *God in Creation: An Ecological Doctrine of Creation*, trans. Margaret Kohl (London: SCM Press, 1985), 2.

[21] Richard Baukham, "Jurgen Moltmann," in *The Modern Theologians*, ed. David F. Ford (Oxford: Blackwell Publishers, 1989), 297.

[22] Ibid.

[23] Ibid., 19.

[24] Jurgen Moltmann, *The Church in the Power of the Holy Spirit* (London: SCM Press, 1977), 315.

[25] Ibid.

[26] Jurgen Moltmann, *History and the Triune God* (New York: Crossroad, 1991), 64.

[27] Ibid.

[28] Grenz, *20th CenturyTheology*, 185.

[29] Moltmann, The *Trinity and the Kingdom of God*, 175.

[30] Moltmann, *God in Creation*, 258.

[31] Ibid., 279.

[32] Moltmann, *Trinity and the Kingdom of God*, 221.

[33] Moltmann, *Church in the Power of the Spirit*, 121.

[34] Ibid., 316.

[35] Ibid.

[36] Ibid., 317.

[37] Ibid.

[38] Ibid., 329.

[39] Ibid., 225-226.

[40] Ibid., 197.

[41] Ibid., 35.

[42] Ibid., 242.

[43] Jurgen Moltmann, *The Crucified God: The Cross as the Foundation and Criticism of Christian Theology* (London: SCM Press, 1974), 44.

[44] Moltmann, *Church in the Power of the Spirit*, 252.

[45] Quoted by Baukham, *The Theology...*, 144.

[46] Baukham, *The Theology of Jurgen Moltmann*, 126.

[47] Moltmann, *Church in the Power of the Spirit*, 2.

[48] Ibid., 105.

[49] Ibid., 134.

[50] Ibid., 11

[51] Jurgen Moltmann, *The Open Church: An Invitation to a Messianic Lifestyle* (London: SCM Press, 1978), 115.

[52] Ibid.

[53] Moltmann, *The Open Church*, 86.

[54] Ibid., 91.

[55] Ibid., 96.

[56] Ibid., 198.

[57] Ibid., 289-290.

[58] Jurgen Moltmann, *The Spirit of Life: A Universal Affirmation*, trans. Margaret Kohl (Minneapolis: Fortress Press, 1992; reprint, 1993), 182.

[59] Ibid., 182.

[60] Jurgen Moltmann, *God for a Secular Society: The Public Relevance of Theology* (Minneapolis: Fortress, 1999), 243.

[61] Moltmann, *Spirit of Life...*, 225.

[62] Jurgen Moltmann, "Pentecost and the Theology of Life," *Concillium* 03 (1996): 132.

[63] Moltmann, *The Spirit of Life...*, 8.

[64] Ibid., 2.

[65] Ibid., 240-241.

[66] Moltmann, "Pentecost...", 131.

[67] Moltmann, *The Spirit of Life...*, 240.

[68] Ibid., 83-143.

[69] Moltmann, *The Church in the Power...*, 330.

[70] Ibid.

[71] Ibid., 330.

[72] Ibid., 331.

CHAPTER-3

# Towards a *Sarvodaya* Ecclesiology

## Introduction

Ecclesiology or the theology of the Church is the articulation of the self-understanding of the Church. This self-understanding is historically, culturally, politically and theologically conditioned. But a critical observation would bring the Church to the seat of judgment because of its inability to render its service to the needs of the people. The first chapter portrayed different nuances of the meaning of community that focused on bonding, goal and *bhakti*-oriented community. The second chapter supplemented these dimensions with a messianic and trinitarian community of friendship from the writings of Moltmann. This chapter would look into the present context of India along with a brief survey of the ecclesiological models in history and insights from the ecclesiology of Moltmann to discover new meaning and relevance for the Indian Church.

## A Brief Analysis on Indian Context

India is a country distinguished by various regional-linguistic-cultural and multi-religious contexts. It is this plural nature that makes India a unique among other civilizations. In order to get a clear picture, it becomes necessary to harvest the different social, political, religious and economic fabric of India thereby locating the Church in the context.

## Unjust Social Setting

Caste system and Patriarchy are the basic social features of the Indian Subcontinent. The caste system provides a hierarchical and compartmental view of society. With this view a whole new system of oppression and marginalization creeps into the society whereby people are not looked on as equals rather as slaves for the masters. Caste system is believed to be instituted by God based on the laws of purity and pollution.[1] With modern and postmodern evolution of humankind in the field of science and technology, it is difficult to find change in the attitude of people towards the lower caste. To phrase it differently, there has been no change in the caste consciousness in the post-independent India. As Felix Wilfred says, "modernity with all its IT revolution and with high profile entrepreneurial and managerial mantras has not changed an iota in the frame of mind that is soaked in caste consciousness."[2]

One of the most affected groups in India due to caste is Dalits. They are denied of living as humans and face discriminations in all walks of life.[3] In spite of the economic, educational and technological development, the intensity of casteism in the 21st century Indian Society can be evident in the anti-reservation agitation in All India Institute of Medical Sciences (AIIMS), New Delhi and in the Sukhadeo Thorat Committee Report on AIIMS. The Thorat committee reports that that due to the harassment from upper caste student groups, Dalits and Tribal students moved out of their hostel rooms to live in cluster among themselves.[4] Now Dalits are on their way to write their own history where they are the subjects of historical reality.[5]

Along with Caste System, the issue of Patriarchy is another social evil that has surmounted the Indian life. Women are discriminated under this system in different levels. They are considered not as the member of the family but as an appendage for satisfying the sexual needs of the men.[6] The Patriarchal culture restricts women the access to education, property and other social privileges. It creates division of labour on gender basis and uses all kinds of social pressures including violence to maintain the status quo especially the oppressive condition of the women.[7] As both of these marginalized groups do not have high rubber of hold in the political arena, their voices are seldom heard in the society. In this context, the Indian Church which highlighted the liberating message of Jesus Christ has to be critically looking into the status of these groups from ecclesial premises.

## Political Context

Just as been observed about the plural nature of the social context so is with the political scenario. There are numerous political parties both in the national and regional level that subscribe to particular agendas. Among these parties some would be in the ruling side and others will be in the opposition. The political parties are carried in the line of serving the people with commitment and total allegiance to the constitution. Though the political movements are based on their respective ideologies, often money, caste, religion and regionalism play fundamental role on the way to attain power. People have lost their trust even on the judiciary because of the corruption and manipulation of justice for the elites.[8] Parliamentary democracy is under the threat of corruption, money power and gun-culture. Instead of the socialist politics, communal politics dominate the political situation of our secular state.[9] The 2G Spectrum scam is the most corrupted deal in the history of Indian politics that has tarnished the image of India and has brought into the dock of shame before the world. The most shameful was when Kapil Sibal, the telecom minister defended that there is no loss to the exchequer of 1,76,000 crore which denied the already proven case by the CAG (Comptroller and Auditor General).[10] Religion and caste based on communal forces often tend to polarize the politics and thereby destroy the moral values of secular politics. Governments that take oath for safeguarding the rights of the people and protect the poor and the oppressed frequently ignore the legitimate demands of the people and support the interest of the rich and influential.[11] Today communal politics provides a new platform for establishing one's supremacy over the other. This can rightly be witnessed in the communal riots in Gujarat and Godhra incidents.[12] The final verdict on the reported confession made recently by swami Aseemananda, leader of Abhinav

Bharat, a Hindutva extremist organization, reveals the fact of these groups spreading terror to counter the Muslim extremism.[13]

Another important aspect of Indian politics is again the dominance of Patriarchy. The patriarchal supremacy that ignores gender equality guaranteed in the constitution can be seen in the delay of passing the Women's Reservation Bill, which provide thirty-three percent of seats for women in the parliament and legislative assembles. Though there are places for women in the Panchayat level but face many problems from the male counterparts.[14] The long-awaited women's bill was materialized only in 2010 with backing from majority of the parties. Today Christian community is seen in the path of communal politics that supports those parties who supports them for vested interest and ignores the wider issues. Therefore, in this desperate situation the need of a community called Church has to overcome the communal politics and re-affirm the values of society without overlooking Jesus' ethics of love, respect and justice irrespective of class, caste and gender.

## Economic Context

Indian economy is considered as one of the growing economies of the world.[15] A large section of people in India live in rural regions. Many of them are farmers, who work in the unorganized sectors and live a life of poverty.[16] Though governments boast over the economic growth in terms of GDP, but seldom recognize the death toll increased in many parts of Indian states by farmers due to heavy loss in their economy.[17] The recent reports of the grains rotting in the storehouses without proper security and lack of proper administration are the prime example of political and economic negligence. Poor people are committing suicide due to their inability to provide for their families. Liberalization in the trade sector, instead of doing benefit for the natives, is becoming the platform for the global business players. As a result, the number of poor people is increasing daily and threatening the very existence of the majority. There is a wide gap between the rich and the poor; the urban and the rural areas in development. Rural poverty increases large scale migration and urbanization which in turn has increased in other problems like land encroachment, increase in murders, thefts etc. Due to the lack of state attention on rural areas, public services such as health care and education have been disintegrated. This has resulted in the increase in malnutrition, increase of new diseases etc. Constitution has strictly put a ban on the child labour but a close involvement in the society will reveal the fact of numerous children working as laborers in the markets.[18] Poverty has become a trend of Indian subcontinent. It is estimated that one in every ten Indians suffers from overt or covert hunger. Three hundred million Indians are still surviving with less than a dollar a day. Though government claims that poverty rates are falling, it is only above one percent a year.[19] Dalits and Tribals are the most affected people owing to Industrialization. Not only their lands have been taken away by the business tycoons, but their very existence has come under question due to the poisoning of the land from the Industrial waste. Sarah Hiddleston put light on issue by investigating the thermometer factory in Kodaikanal, owned by Hindustan Unilever.[20] Because of the privatization policy in the public sector, the

Dalits lose their reservation privileges. Since Dalits do not get quality education, they are not able to enjoy the benefits of globalization. Special Economic Zones are the new phenomenon of globalization that has put the life of farmers and poor in total chaos.[21] The aforementioned analysis provides a surgical impression of flaws in the economic policies and developmental projects that claim to function for the upliftment of the poor and the marginalized. In the midst of all the structural evils often the faith communities stand as mute spectators legitimizing it.

## Prejudiced Religious Scenario

Indian society is a religiously pluralistic society. Different religious traditions co-exist and promote the value of freedom, love and integrity of human beings. But the secular society which is religiously sensitive has been disturbed by communalism. It poses a tremendous threat to the nation's secular philosophy i.e. unity, justice and fraternity. Majority and minority communalism equally disturb the communal harmony and create hatred among the people of diverse religious traditions. Minority communalism is interpreted as separation and secession while majority communalism breeds brutal and sustained repression of the minorities. Today, religion is politicized for communal interest.[22] The most vulnerable groups in India, in terms of religion, are the Dalits and Tribals. They are considered as impure and polluted. They are not only the victim of religio-philosophical interpretation but also are used by different fundamental forces to oppress minority communities. The Hindutva forces often divide people based on religious traditions.[23] Ashgar Ali Engineer opines that the riots in Bhilwada, Rajasthan on 30th December show the attempt of Sangh Pariwar in converting Rajasthan to another Gujarat.[24] Also they create enmity between the Christian Dalits and Tribals with their brothers belonging to other religion.[25] Even though religious freedom is guaranteed by the Indian Constitution, Dalits and Tribals are deprived of the freedom because of communal forces. Anti-conversion bills are targeted against their conversion.

The call for minority rights is another trend in the religious context of India. Usually if there is any communal violence, the political parties and minority communities uphold minority rights to bring the attention of governments to protect the minority communities. Today, the emphasis on minority rights has reduced to protect the rights and privileges of minorities especially the management of educational institutions. If the government interferes in the affairs of minority educational institutions to ensure transparent dealings regarding admission and appointment, the minority communities especially the Christians raise voice for minority rights. The Christian Church in Kerala fought with government in its attempt to control the self-financing professional colleges. They even issue pastoral letters to all their parishes against the government.[26] Minority communities of West Bengal also conducted mass rally under the banner of United Minority Forum against the government interference in the management of minority institutions.[27] In short, religion has been politicized for communal interest, and life realities of people have not been the concern of faith communities. Church has become a communal entity that advocates for communal interest without critically engaging in the struggles of the common people.

The above section has briefly pointed out the flaws in our Indian ethos that has become the victim of western ideologies and globalization. The Indian social virtue that has been the mark of the Indian community that was based on respect, dignity and mutuality is now in the path of moral deterioration stamped with self-interest. The religious context has exposed the naked reality of how religion has become the handmaid for political end and has stained the democratic lawsuit with innocent blood. The political scenario has witnessed the gang rape of human rights at every instance without locking the real culprit behind the bars. It also confirms the manipulation of justice for the cause of the elites by the judiciary who are supposed to be the last resort of the common people. It has also brought out the dark reality of Church that knowingly either taken the path of silence or has become the facilitators of oppression. In this context what should be the true nature of the Church? What was the nature of the Church in History with its own contextual issues? Was it a communal force or a community of the people? A critical analysis of the ecclesiological models in the next section would throw some light into the nature of the Church in history.

## Historical Development in the Models of Ecclesiology

Ecclesiology is a branch of systematic theology that studies the identity, nature, unity and mission of the church. Church as it seen today with all its detailed structures, doctrines and rituals is not explicitly instituted by Jesus, rather it a product of historical development. In New Testament Greek, the most common word for Church is *ekklesia,* meaning "assembly."[28] In classical Greek literature, the citizens of a city are called out by a herald, who summons them to come together as community. Thus, the term *ekklesia* has an official connotation since the people were to assemble for officially sanctioned purposes.[29] *Ekklesia* is translated from two common Hebrew terms *Qahal* and *Edhah*[30] for the gathering of the people. *Qahal* is the assembly of Israel convoked by God (Deut. 5:19, 23:2-9; Num 16:3; Micah 2:5). There is also a theological significance for the term *ekklesia* as it expressed the claim of the Christian community in the face of the world.[31] In short, it refers to a gathering of community in a secular world. What was the context of the secular world at the time of Jesus?

## Social Milieu

Palestine at the time of Jesus was undergoing a deep crisis due to centuries of colonial rule one after the other, first by the Persians, then the Greeks and lastly by the Romans. This led the country to an economic crisis that made large part of the people of Palestine landless, unemployed, poor, sick, crippled, lame and possessed. Cultural and religious imperialism of the colonial rulers caused a still more serious and much deeper cultural and religious crisis which deeply affected the psyche of the people.[32] Jesus came to the midst of such a people to whom he proclaimed the "Good News" of total liberation. Thus, the community of Jesus was a reaction to the socio-cultural-political and religious demands of the context. The community model became a necessity for the Church to spread the kingdom values and affirm their identity in the New Testament period.

## Church in the New Testament: A Community of Love and Sharing

The New Testament does not give an explicit, systematic and detailed picture of Church at its origins. Among the evangelists it is Mathew who gives some details about the life of the early Christian community (Mt 18:1-20)[33]: The Church was a community of "little ones," a fellowship of brothers and sisters, a community of equals, where Jesus alone was the Master. But Jesus himself came not "to be served but to serve." The leadership in the community was one of service. In matters of policies and decisions the community had the last word, not any individual leader. It is Jesus' presence, living and dynamic presence, which makes the Church what it is (Mt 18:20). He did not establish an elite community as opposed to the religions of his day. Pannenberg opines, "Jesus did not find a fellowship of followers separate from the rest of the people but proclaimed to the whole people the nearness of his God."[34] Acts of Apostles mentions the unifying elements of the early Christian community: the teaching of the Apostles, fellowship, the breaking of bread and prayer (Acts 2:42-47; 4:32-35; 5:2-12). These early Christian communities, their gathering and celebrations were the signs of the coming of the Kingdom of God which was witnessed in the miracles of Jesus. It was a Kingdom community anticipated as divine-human movement for the human community to respond.[35] In the words of Moltmann, it is a messianic community where the believers participate in the mission of Christ towards the eschatological

Kingdom.[36] Theologically speaking, Church represents Kingdom community, where people respond to the coming Kingdom of God with a transformed heart by the unconditional love of God, create a new community where there is total freedom, fellowship and justice. In short, Church in the New Testament was based on community model. But G.S.M Walker opines that though community model can be witnessed in the New Testament but does not feature a single unique ecclesiology, as no New Testament writer uses the *ekklesia* in a collective way.[37]

In the Pauline letters, the *ekklesia* refers to the local churches and each local congregation is considered as a Church in a collective way. The Church is conceived as organic where each community however small represents the total community, the Church."[38] Paul considers the body of each believer as a temple of God. This is a growing entity living with the life of Christ himself. "We are to grow in every way into him who is the head, that is into Christ from whom the whole body joined and knit together by every joint…grows bodily and builds up in love (Eph 3: 15-16; 4:12-13; Col 2:19)."[39] Here the image of body has moved to the corporate understanding with Christ as lord over that body (Eph4: 4-5). In Romans 12 and I Corinthians 12, the main point is the mutual union, mutual concern and mutual dependence of the members of the local community upon one another for the service of the community which can be spotted in different vocation introduced by Paul (like apostle, prophets, evangelist, pastors and teachers that would suffice the cause of the community Eph 4:11), which later took an institutional form in the pastoral epistles.[40]

However, in general, Paul's understanding of the church tends to be more organic, communitarian and mystical. Therefore, the New Testament community did not project a systematic religious sentiment rather it was a community based on love, equality and service.

## Church in the Early Period: Communitarian to Hierarchical

The ministerial offices inaugurated by Paul in his epistles took a major shift in the later years. The ministerial office for the community building was developed into hierarchical office. This was due to the external and internal threats that lurked at the door of Christian community. The external threat was from the Roman Empire who persecuted and threatened the very existence of the believing community which resulted in the migration to various places and formed local churches. The situation forced the believers to maintain unity under a leadership which paved the way for Bishop-centered Christianity. Thus, the model of 'perfect society' was defined with rules and regulation, assumed a pyramidal structure. Pope became the Vicar of Christ and authority for salvation.[41] The Gnostics, Mystery religions and other philosophical traditions raised the internal threat.[42] Origen's and Cyprian's dictum of salvation is only in the Church administered by the Bishops, was directed against the Gnostics and other schismatic.[43] Against the Gnostics, Irenaeus taught that "the Church is the unique sphere of the Holy Spirit possessing the canon of truth in apostolic succession focused in the Roman Church."[44] Augustine, in reaction to the Donatist held on the one hand that Church is a fellowship of love; on the other hand, it is a mixed community of good and bad under the rule of one, holy Catholic Church.[45] When Christianity became a state religion with the conversion of Constantine in 313,[46] the Church was defined as the 'one holy, catholic and apostolic church' in the Nicene Constantinopolitan creed of 325 and 381 respectively.[47] All the Churches in the early period were characterized by the presence of offices for its own function independent of others. J.N.D Kelly writes, "looked at from the outside, primitive Christianity has a vast diffusion of local congregation each leading separate life with its own constitutional structure and office and each called a Church."[48] In short, Origen, Cyprian, Irenaeus were the advocate of Church as a universal institution for salvation.

Against this institutional hierarchical model many movements came forward. One such movement came from Montanus who was against the organized Church. He says, "The Spirit was suppressed by the organized Church."[49] The Montanist reaction against the ecclesiastical fixation of Christianity runs throughout Church history in one form or another. Therefore, clear shift from a communitarian model to a more institutional model is witnessed in the development of the Church in history.

### The Medieval Period: Communitarian to Secularized

The Medieval Church[50] tried to identify itself with the Kingdom of God in terms of the hierarchical graces. Pope Gregory VII argued that the *Ecclesia Romana* was founded by God alone because it is the Pope who is the successor of Peter, and gradually this led to the establishment of the Church under

Papal monarchy.[51] The Church made sacraments as absolutely essential for salvation and people cannot be saved without the Church and the priests thereby exerting a great tyranny over souls and conscience for centuries.[52] Since the Medieval Church was under the clutches of the hierarchical authority, a series of initiatives were headed by committed believers to find out the real meaning of Christian fellowship. The Church allied with the state power employing both force and persuasion and sought to restrain the emerging movements.[53] Monastic movement emerged as a symbolic expression of the devotional life of the medieval believers. The intention behind this movement was formation of an improvised Church in place of the corrupted institutionalized Church.[54] 'Mysticism' became a new trend that emphasized on contemplation and a mystical union of human soul with the infinite.[55] But it did not attack the Church openly and later became a handmaid of the Church. Through this movement the laity was given greater participation and insights into the nature of Christianity.[56] Another movement 'Joachimism' related to the teachings of Joachim of Fiore was a protest against the Pope centered hierarchical and secularized Church brought by Gregorian reform in the 11$^{th}$ century. They believed that the new age of the Holy Spirit, an egalitarian of freedom and love was imminent. He looked for the emergence of a new "spiritual church" to supersede the old church of Pope, priests, sacraments, biblical doctrines and theological creeds.[57]

The self-understanding of the Church along the imperial and political model as a hierarchically and highly secularized and structured institution with uniformity, centralization, jurisdiction and absolute power was met with division in the Church. It was divided into East and West with their respective languages, customs and culture. Due to the Western imposition of the beliefs on the East, particularly the 'filioque' clause finally separated them in 1054, which is called the great schism of the East.[58] Thus, the Church which started as liberated community was soon imprisoned by the hierarchical society which finally resulted in schism. The institutional nature of Church was then confronted by Martin Luther in the form of Reformation.

## Reformation: A Subversion of Institutionalized *Ecclesia*

In the 14th century, complaints about the tyranny of Rome and its insatiable hunger for money, and the widespread spiritual and moral decay of the clergy led to the first vigorous call for reform.[59] Reformers like Martin Luther, John Calvin and Ulrich Zwingli and so on, raised their voices against the aberration in the Church and called for reform.[60] Luther stressed the non-institutional nature of the Church. He disliked the word *Kirche* (Church) and preferred the term *Sammlung* (assembly) and *Gememeinde* (congregation).[61] For him, *ecclesia*, however, ought to mean the holy Christian people, not only of the time of apostles, who are since dead, but clear to the end of the world, so that there is always living on earth a Christian holy people in which Christ lives, works, and reigns through grace and forgiveness of sins.[62] William Estep observes that Luther wishfully implemented the concept of Free Church, according to which Churches would be comprised of committed Christians who voluntarily formed fellowship for the purpose of mutual edification and service.[63] Here love, concern and fellowship with others as community is important than structures or doctrines. But the historical reality of the Church was not addressed by Luther who gave more attention to the Word of God. Modern issues in the modern era compelled the Church to deal with realities of the time and the context seriously. This resulted in the re-visioning of the Church in many traditions.

## Re-visioning of the Church in Modernity

Various social, political and religious reform movements influenced the modern Church to rethink about some of its theological self-understanding. This section will be a brief critical look into some of the ecclesiological models in the post- Reformation period.

## Roman Catholic Model

The basic characteristic of the earlier ecclesiology was centered on papacy and reflected a 'contract-based community.'[64] Prior to Vatican II, the Church was portrayed as the only hope of Salvation. Vatican I (1871) championed a predominantly hierarchical view of Church. But Vatican II became more people oriented and describe Church "as a mystery or sacrament, as the whole people of God, as a collegial reality... as having a mission not only to proclaim the Kingdom of God in word and sacrament, but to be itself a credible sign and example of that kingdom as well as an instrument of its realization in the world at large through its service on behalf of justice and peace."[65] With the dynamic "people of God" notion in which Church is seen first of all as a pilgrim people on the way to the heavenly city."[66] It is the Spirit of God that constitutes the journey of the pilgrim people of God and supersedes any structures and offices of the Church. As Rahner writes, the Spirit is constitutive of the Church in a way more basic than its institutional structure.[67] Also change in the view was the acceptance of other churches as carrying the salvific function. As Pope John Paul II in his encyclical on ecumenism, *ut unum sint*[68] gives importance to the unity and it can be realized only when those who invoke the triune God and confess Jesus as Lord and savior.[69] This confession brings people into a community with equal heart, mind and commitment. As John Fuellanbach writes, "'Love, acceptance, forgiveness, commitment, and intimacy constitute the Church's very fabric.'[70] It is 'a community in which justice, peace and mutual love are realized and lived.'[71] For Yves Congar, church becomes relevant only when it exists in community, communion and fellowship of humanity. [72] It is a fellowship of men, women and children with God and with one another in Christ. Thus, Catholic ecclesiology replaced a hierarchical ecclesiology to a more community-based ecclesiology. This change was to defend their religious territory and establish peace and harmony.

But the disadvantage in this ecclesiology is its inability to provide lay participation in the community. As in 1st Peter 2:5 it says that all those who are in Christ belong to holy priesthood so is the Church, a place where believers exercise their freedom for the glory of God. This model provides an obscurity of the cooperation between the spiritual and the visible dimensions of the Church, the danger of divinizing the Church beyond its due, the lack of clarity regarding the Church's identity and mission and the possibility of reducing the Church to a social impulse. Though it has given importance to the role of Holy Spirit in the community life, but it has failed to promote its expression and function in the edification of individual's life. It does not provide any strong motivation for missionary work. There is some unresolved tension between the Church as a network of friendly interpersonal relationships and the Church as a communion of grace. Members of close communities may feel at home only among themselves and regard others as outsiders and intruders. This model also fails to depict the dynamics of the fellowship in a community which can be witnessed in the next model of ecclesiology i.e. Eastern Orthodox ecclesiology.

## Eastern Orthodox Model

For Eastern Christianity, church is understood as the image of Trinity. Just as each person is made in the image of Trinity, so the Church as a whole is an icon of the Trinity "reproducing on earth the mystery of unity in diversity."[73] However John Zizioulas cautions, "Church is not a sort of Platonic 'image' of the Trinity; she is communion in the sense of being the people of God, Israel, and the 'body of Christ,' i.e. in the sense of serving and realizing herself God's purpose in history for the sake of entire creation."[74] The image of Trinity is present not only in the Church but also in other communities and institutions as well.[75] Kallistos Ware vociferously points out the characteristics of Trinity as of identity and mutuality in simultaneous activity without hampering one's uniqueness. He says, "In the Trinity the three are one God, yet each is fully personal; in the Church a multitude of human persons is united in one, yet each preserves her or his personal diversity

unimpaired. The mutual indwelling of the persons of the Trinity
is paralleled by the coherence of the members of the Church."[76]
It is in the Church that human beings are restored to their
original role as co-creator with God. Paulos Mar Gregorios in
line with the Cappadocian fathers expounds the term *energia*
or energy through which people participate in the work of
God.[77] Eucharistic meal stands as a symbol of participation
through Christ in the work of God. The underlying fact of this
Eucharistic communion is the presence of the Holy Spirit. In
Short, Church becomes the icon when Christ and Spirit work
simultaneously in communion with the will of the father to
form a community of relationship.

The weakness of this ecclesiology is that it makes
communion an internal affair of the Church with partial
indication to believer's spiritual life in the community. The
participation in the Church as community seldom recognizes
the value of each individual in the community building and
fulfilling the needs of those deserving. One major problem
that is been observed is the lack of addressing the issue of sin
in the lives of believers which might hamper the community
life. This issue is seriously dealt in the next model.

## Lutheran Model[78]

Luther stressed the non-institutional character of the Church.
On the one hand, against the catholic position that regards the
Church/hierarchy as absolute; on the other hand, against the
enthusiasts who appealed to be the custodians of the Holy
Spirit and therefore true reformers.[79] He disliked the word *Kirche*
and preferred terms such as *Sammlung* (assembly) and *Gemeinde*

(congregation). For him Church in the first place is a communion of saints, a gathering of believers.[80] It implies that Church is not an institution for the supply of blessing, rather it is the communion of believers where gospel is proclaimed, and Lords table is commemorated. Church is something that is going on in the world.[81] Luther also provided a strong idea of the Priesthood of all believers which is the continuation of early Church and Middle ages. According to him, sharing in Jesus Christ on the basis of baptism includes also the sharing in his priesthood. Christ bearing the burdens and interceding for believers' cause is a priestly work; so also, is the participation and service in the Church a priestly activity.[82] In other words, the priesthood of Christ shares the priesthood of all Christians. This understanding of the priesthood undercuts the hierarchical vision of the Church and liberates the Church from subjection to hierarchical authority.

What about the sinners in the Church when it is called the priesthood of all believers? Luther answers this by saying that believers are just and sinful simultaneously (simul Justus et peccator). This Church of Christ, the communion of saints, is also always a communion of sinners until the Lord returns. In other words, ecclesiastical purity is not a moral but a functional phenomenon. As long as the Church is guided by the Holy Spirit, mediated by the Word and sacrament, it will remain pure.

The limitation of this ecclesiology is Luther's unclarified statement about the sinners in the Church as a functional phenomenon while negating the moral aspect of a believer. He calls therefore, the Church as incomplete. This has been misinterpreted by many in the Church and therefore, immoral elements have slowly crept into the Church. This model fails to promote the parameters of leading a saintly life in the context of committing a deliberate sin. Emphasis on the impossibility of salvation by merit sometimes led to an exaggerated interpretation of original sin as involving the total absence of good in man. It led to a doctrine of election which saddled God with the arbitrary will to save some and to leave others equally undeserving of his favour to perish eternally. It also led to the legalism of the Word of God and idolatry in the sacramentalism.[83]

## Pentecostal/Charismatic[84] Model

Is there a Pentecostal ecclesiology at all? Except M.L. Hodge and Peter Hocken, there is little contribution from the Pentecostal theologians to the concept of Church, since most Pentecostals emphasize the spiritual and invisible nature of the Church. Much of their writings have been on ecclesiastical polity that is characterized by the apostolic legacy.[85] They move away from traditional hierarchical structure to a more participative form. Pentecostal spirituality and theology have almost from the start appreciated 'fellowship' language over 'institutionalized Church.' Pentecostals view the Church as a charismatic fellowship, a pneumatologically constituted reality. In short, it is an ecclesiology of the fellowship of persons experienced in the community through the power of Holy Spirit. They quote 1 Cori 12:13 which portray the New Testament picture of the Church: 'Fellowship was a common experience of baptism into the body of Christ through the Spirit.[86] This fellowship is something to be experienced, a shared experience in the everyday life of the community. As Leslies Newbigin says that a real congregational life, wherein each member has their own opportunity to contribute to the life of the whole body through gifts which the Spirit endows him/her, is as much part of the essence of the Church as are ministry and sacrament.[87] In this community life there is no discrimination entertained and all are welcome to participate in the ministry of the Church.

The limitation with Pentecostal ecclesiology is its over emphasis on the Holy Spirit that keeps the other members of the Trinity at bay. It is observed that any member who possesses gifts of the Spirit tends to claim himself/herself as authoritative, splits from the mother Church and starts a new Church. The lack of discipline and structure paves the way for this kind of problems. Another aspect is the issue of individualism that has crept into the Church where believers only think in terms of their spiritual well-being while ignoring the pathos of fellow believers. The understanding of the free flow ministry of the Holy Spirit often tends the Pentecostal meeting to end up in disorder. Earlier when people were separated owing to their caste and class consciousness are now divided based on the exercise of the spiritual gifts. Church should neither be a platform of showcasing community's administrative strength nor a channel of spiritual catharsis invoked by entertainment buzz rather it should be a community that spearhead the process of spiritual edification in the life of individual and the Church should participate in the death and resurrection or passion and joy of Christ. The community centered fellowship that vociferously segregates itself from other traditional Church is brought together in the next model.

## Ecumenical Model

One of the creative contributions to the ecclesiological models of the Church comes from the Ecumenical movement. The purpose and agenda of Ecumenical movement in principle states 'it is the community of all those who believe in Christ, and so it purports to promote the unity of Christians and Churches.[88] It is argued that if the Church is the Church of Christ, and since there is only one Christ, then unity belongs to the nature of the Church. In other words, the unity of the Church is not a human effort, but a God given gift to all Christians. Pannenberg argues that it is not only the community of all believers but also of all humanity. For Hans Kung, the ecumenism extends even to the other religious traditions.[89] In order to achieve this, the ecumenists assert that Communion model could be appropriate to this task. The underlying current for this attempt can be realized through communion of the persons of Trinity which stands as the highest and loftiest expression of unity for Christians. The communion is not intended for gaining organizational uniformity rather establishing a unity with all its differences and uniqueness. Vandervelde says that the character of this communion is to zero on unacceptable division, while at the same time acknowledging the measure of unity that does exist within diversity.[90] This affirmation can be seen in 'The Final Report' (1985-1989) of the International Dialogue between Roman Catholic and the Pentecostals. The concept of communion is the recent trend of ecclesiological development which can be witnessed among the Orthodox Church, the Lutheran Church and other Protestant Churches and even among the Free Churches.[91] Ecumenical ecclesiology looks closely towards the role of Holy Spirit in the unity of Churches. The Church is a Communion in the Spirit since it is in the Spirit that all Christians are united together as one Church.[92] In short, what is imperative in this communion through Spirit is the founding of a community of whole inhabited earth. Having said this, how the ecumenism can be openly materialized in the ongoing tension prevailing in the Christian denominations? What is that aspect which can bind every Church together in one knot without diffusing its uniqueness? Moltmann asserts that it is under the cross of Christ that all Christians come together because it is the cross that reminds us of being brothers and sisters in the same poverty and imprisoned in sin, burden of guilt and emptiness of hearts. We do not stand under the cross as Protestants, as Catholics, or as Orthodox and Pentecostals rather as godless who are justified, enemies are reconciled the poor are enriched....[93]

Among these positive attempts, there are some discrepancies in this ecclesiology. The communion model though has created an amicable relation among different major Church traditions and establish various ecumenical meetings and conferences but has failed to promote an organic unity that was envisioned. Ecumenists are unclear about the Church which focuses on the community of whole inhabited earth can be called a Church anymore. How would Ecumenism solve the issue of other religion's claim of better community than the Church? Paulos Mar Gregorios observes that Ecumenical councils still represent the framework of western ecclesiology rather than working on creative indigenous ecclesial unity.[94] It also isolates the question of unity from the question of truth i.e. How the Word of God be a parameter for all communities. Due to the lack of proper ecumenical guidelines people are still confused of visible unity with uniformity which can be clearly witnessed in the attitude of Pentecostals towards Ecumenism in India.

## Feminist Model

The main task of Feminist ecclesiology is to dismantle the model of Church as 'household ruled by a patriarch' and replace it with a model of 'household where everyone gathers around a common table to break bread and share table talk and hospitality.'[95] Letty Russell proposes a symbolism of table to create new images of the Church. Table symbolizes hospitality and sharing. It speaks of God's hospitality and inclusive attitude. The "Church around the table" is a "discipleship of equals."[96] This fellowship is "connective"; there is a living, dynamic connection between men and women and between God and Human beings. Russell argues, 'If the table is spread by God and hosted by Christ, it must be a table with many connections."[97] Fiorenza held that the earliest Christian movement was thoroughly egalitarian and that the patriarchal pattern of male domination came late into the 1st century Church as an accommodation to Roman Church. As Jesus' community was built on the principle of egalitarianism, so also the feminist Church looks to develop a paradigmatic community of women where they are held in equality with men in all aspect of ecclesial life. Consequently, "the women-identified man Jesus called forth a discipleship of equals that still needs to be discovered and realized by women and men today."[98] Feminist ecclesiology would consider leadership not as pyramidycal;

rather they affirm the partnership paradigm that is oriented towards community formation in the line of Jesus' kingdom values.[99]

The problem with this ecclesiology is that it claims to represent the universal women and their problems but practically speaking has led down many women of different cultural origins. The biggest challenge for this model lies in its inability to implicate the partnership paradigm to the male saviour Christ, the head of the Church. When it is table fellowship where all are held equal how Christ, who is a male, is taken as the head of the table? Though Feminist theologians have done great service by purging away the evils of patriarchy from the Christian community, but it also provides a new schism within the body of Christ. It has also failed to sketch the norm for criticizing its own principles i.e. self-criticism. It has rightly brought out the importance of history in constructing theological premises which was denied by many modern theologians.

## Ecclesiology in the writings of selected Indian Christian Theologians

Indian Christian Theology was necessitated under the context of strong criticism raised against the western import of theological expression practiced in Indian context. Almost all the theologians had a critical approach towards the western ecclesiology. Among them only three Indian theologians would be taken for understanding how Church is understood in the Indian context. They are Pandippedi Chenchiah, Sebastian Kappen and M.M. Thomas. These theologians would suite the researcher's argument on community and provide different dimension which other theologians' understanding of Church would be sufficed within their concepts.

## 1.    Ecclesiology of Pandippedi Chenchiah

Chenchiah was vociferously rallied against the traditional ecclesiology. Coming to the Church from a Hindu background he found it oppressively alien and western, introspective and quarrelsome, more interested in administration than in the Christian life.[100] The Church in the West has virtually become a department of the state and an instrument for maintaining the power and the prosperity of the privileged class. He opines that, "Church was born out of the exigencies of early Christianity when it was confronted with the highly organized imperial society that was in Rome."[101] Christianity became a state religion by conquering Rome and consolidated a community based on a political front of power. He writes, "As a movement, Christians conquered Rome; as a community they were conquered by Rome…. If a religion becomes the victim of community, a sect or a caste, then that religion cannot hold the spiritual potential for the time. He therefore, concluded that it was essential to find new and vital forms of Christian community and turned to the ancient Hindu idea of the *Ashram*, a small community of faithful people living a life of the greatest simplicity, usually as disciples of a master. For him, "the ashrams are the small circles which reflect the fullness of Christian life. An ashram is a Christian group that comes nearest to the true conception of the church-which should be a family."[102] Every Ashram should endeavour to reproduce Jesus in the lives of inmates.[103] The Ashram is more biblical than the western conception of the Church. He says, "The ashram will rescue the Christians from the bondage of law, under which the church seeks to bring the Christian under negation of the Pauline injunction: if you are led by the Spirit you are no longer under the law."[104] What he envisages for India is a 'religionless' Christianity without ritual sacraments, creeds and confessions. He says, "There will be no baptisms, no confessions of faith, no creedal profession... [The Hindu] will slowly and in different degrees come under the influence of the Spirit of Christ, without change or nomenclature... The change will be in the realm of Spirit-not in the region of *nama* and *rupa*."[105]

Though Ashram model of Chenchiah brings radical discontinuity with the conventional models and take into account the very contextual approach to the Church but fails to satisfy the needs of the subaltern groups like Dalits and Tribals. Dalit and Tribal theologians are strictly against any subscription from the Hindu religious thought because of its Brahmanical elements that binds the lower caste people under the folds of Varna system. Also, Ashram model that has its root from Ashrama dharma cannot be an agent of equality as it tends to exhort but in reality, it will never see the subaltern with equality. Therefore, a community of Jesus Christ needs to take a stand to address the issue of equality, fraternity and justice.

## Ecclesiology of Sebastian Kappen

Kappen's reflection on the Church comes from his observation of the Indian Church that has often found itself irrelevant and obsolete in the context of pre-capitalist and capitalist India. In order to achieve the values, the Church needs to restructure itself from the old value that has decayed the function of the Church. The pre-capitalist India is marked by group solidarity, authority of the guru, kingship, caste status, personal dependence and patronage. And the capitalist values represent individual interest, competition, quantity, consumption of the superfluous and machine.[106] It is this system of values which shapes the faithful to the hierarchy and bourgeois. If Church needs to be relevant, then it cannot be silent and assimilate itself to the order of the world rather it should work for the free and full development of the individual and the community together. He says, "A change over to a radically new set of values will call for a radical restructuring of the Church.[107] It is not a restructuring in the sense of mere rearranging of old elements but a demolition of the old in view of a new creation. With these observation and criticism Kappen asserts the need of a Church that would be holistic and follow the vision and mission of Jesus. Kappen starts his explanation by exploring into Jesus' vision for community. Jesus, who encountered God, was gripped by the vision of human-divine community of the end-time.[108] Jesus required his disciples to seek the Kingdom of God and its justice which is beyond any particularistic, nationalist overtones. It is a Kingdom of new humanity. In short, the message of Jesus made the emergence of a radically new vision of the ultimate possibility open to mankind.[109] It implies that the community of Jesus does not envisage a pattern based on exclusivism and sectarianism but a table fellowship with social outcastes and others who were marginalized in the society. It will be open to all those who look forward to the reign of God and seek to do God's will. As Jesus says, 'whoever does the will of God is my brother, my sister and my mother.'[110]

Kappen enrolls this fellowship as the community of Jesus. The significance of this community according to Kappen is the ability to present the Jesus of yesterday into the present of all those who are oppressed today.[111] It means that Kappen is interested in presenting a more existential ecclesiology for Jesus' followers. Concerning the nature of community, he says that Jesus' community is not just about gathering of believers, rather it is the community of pilgrims who are in a journey beyond themselves towards God.[112] This is the journey of new humanity who are centered on the vision and faith of Jesus Christ, without any attitude of distinction. This community is not about who is superior, rather it is a community of equals. Moltmann call this the community of friendship and fellowship where all are equal.[113] In other words, it was in community in solidarity with and in relation to others, not a community opposed to others.

Kappen's thought on the church is very crucial and practical but his idea of discipleship has left some loopholes to be dealt with. The idea of discipleship portrays the fact of hierarchy between the student and the master. Whatever the master teaches the student has to learn and practice without much freedom. Therefore, applying this concept would again lead us to the conventional methods. Another aspect that Kappen brought is the concept of Kingdom community. The term Kingdom always presupposes a place or state ruled by the king over his people which never connote a sense of equality rather automatically bringing us to a kingly rule saturated with kingly power. Therefore, India with its variety of culture and religion need to be more cautious in developing a Church to address the sensitivity of the people.

## M.M. Thomas Ecclesiology

M.M. Thomas gave his ecclesiological reflection in the context of flowering modernization which was penetrated by the religious, cultural and spiritual ethos of Indian sub-continent. The modern cultural awakening, which was flagged by the renaissance in other religions, secular movements and ideologies, tends to be the cornerstone of any ecclesial mandate. He says, "I would maintain that this Cultural Revolution which is taking place with all its spiritual impact behind it is relevant to the gospel to the Christian mission."[114] Therefore Church as the substrate of Humanism would create a community of humanity that walks in the vision of Jesus. In order to be relevant in the context of modernization, Thomas proposes that Church should welcome a community of 'New Humanity.' He says, "Church is the foretaste and prophetic sign of the New Humanity created in Christ. The Church must be present wherever renewal of humanity takes place."[115]

He opines that the purpose of theology is salvific action, which is the "spiritual inwardness of true humanization," and that "humanization is inherent in the message of salvation in Christ."[116] So Jesus Christ is the source and foundation of true humanization. He writes that what is to be aimed at is a further transformation of "their humanism and their theology in the light of God's purpose for man as revealed in the divine humanity of Jesus Christ."[117] It is only in Christ that one can break the dividing walls of hostility in the name of religion and participate in the nation building. He asserts "Christ is breaking down the wall of partition between Christians and non-Christians, as he did once the partition wall between Jews and Gentiles."[118]

How can Church experience the New humanity? Church's mission is to exercise the new humanity of Christ which is the spiritual foundation, the source of Judgement, renewal and ultimate fulfillment of the struggles of humankind today for its humanity.[119] Therefore experiencing the liberation in the process of humanization would require being rooted in their own contextual demands and entering in dialogue so as to enrich common human values. The dialogue should be based on "Christ-centered syncretism" that would enable Christians to be open to interpenetration at cultural and religious levels, but with Jesus Christ as the principle of discrimination and coherence.[120] As Moltmann rightly says that it is in dialogue and co-operation that Church would fulfill the messianic vocation.[121] He says that the new situation calls for a new Christological understanding of common humanity, with its entire secular and religious dimension, and of the life and mission of Church in relation to how other religious and secular ideological communities of faith are in God's scheme of salvation and will be consummated in God's Kingdom.[122] Therefore his ecclesiology is flavored by Christ with pluralism as its garnish.

His Christ-centered ecclesiology raises some practical problems in the multi-religious context which is responded by some theologians. Abraham Stephen asks, in what way does the new humanity transcend the Church i.e. if the Church is a body of Christ-a people of God for a special purpose- how could Christ transcends the Church? Is Christ the saviour of the world or only a source of humanization? His Christ centeredness appears to represent a form of cultural chauvinism.[123] Bishop Newbigin criticizes Thomas' doctrine of the Church as docetic. Thomas says that a proper theology of the ecclesiology requires a full acknowledgement of Christ in all spheres of social life. Newbigin asks: What did Thomas mean by expression such as "a Christ centered secular fellowship outside the Church" and "a Christ centered fellowship, of faith and ethics in the Hindu religious community?" Can we equate humanization with evangelization?"[124]

## Dalit Ecclesiology

Indian Church is both theologically and in its physical and sociological reality, "the Church of the Dalits" because it constitutes more than 60% of the Indian Christians. But still Church in India projects the Brahmanical preference or the elitist image. Church in India follows the Brahmanical model of Church in line with the Christendom model of the Roman Church. If the Church in India wishes to play a meaningful role in the lives of the Dalit, then it has to abandon the traditional Brahmanical model and baptize itself into the realities of Dalits. James Massey proposes an 'incarnational model' based on John 1:11-4 and Luke 2:1-7, that would cover the entire Dalit issues and is oriented towards the re-visioning of a Dalit community. This model would see God dealing with the Dalit situation by himself becoming an ordinary human being, one who, according to Isaiah, "had no form or comeliness" (53:4).[125] This act of God brought God into complete solidarity with the Dalits. God became the poorest of poor as a human being- God became a Dalit- in order to make all the Dalits of this world rich (2 Cori 8:9). It is an exodus community that had been marginalized for hundreds of years now moving into a new horizon of freedom. Church should not only come out of oppressed situation but also should undertake a prophetic role to drive out the evils of caste. As Amaladoss says, "the Church needs to prophecy to speak to the people in the name of God and in the name of Jesus, a Dalit the liberator."[126] The Challenge is to face the oppressive forces within the Christian community and society at large. A prophetic denunciation of the oppressive situation of Dalits, and all oppressed, means also being ready for conflict with oppressive forces and stressing justice and love for true transformation.[127] Moltmann would say that it is only through the cross the God's future is anticipated, in his suffering solidarity with those who are excluded and forgotten by affluent optimism.[128] But a critical observation would cater the fact that in the Dalit Church itself the Dalits are divided based on class and literacy and becoming the source of oppression in the 21st century. Though Dalit model of Church envisage a Church for all people, but it seldom recognizes the people belonging to other oppressed groups.

## Tribal Ecclesiology

Tribal community revolved around the concept of 'community home', constructed by the united, voluntary labour of the village, located in the heart of the village, near the chief's house. The leader of the local community is responsible for the administration of community home to arrange for all works to be done by inmates in the events of war, death, celebration and accidents. Discipline was strictly enforced in all community homes.[129] Tribal community is best known for their sociability and equality. Sociability means "being together" either for work or for celebration.[130] The basis of this community is communicative. The communication is central to the well-being of the community as it helps to protect the village at the time of war and celebrate at the time of happiness. The function of the community home was protection of village, training young people, and forum for discussing issues, recreation and fellowship.[131] Tribal ecclesiology looks forward to resuscitating the community home concept which was lost due to the onslaught of modernization and furnish the nature of Church in the tribal context. The community home was necessary for strengthening the local community for a transformed reality towards the harmony, welfare and peace. Tribal community would see Church as the community home that act as an agent of transformation towards universal human community through transforming the local community. Though Tribal ecclesiology envisions for a universal community but seldom entertain other denomination or community. The missionaries had influenced them in such a way that they have accommodated into themselves a western form of Church replacing their indigenous nature. Almost all tribal communities are patriarchal in nature and consider women as underprivileged and secondary.

## Ecclesiology of Jurgen Moltmann

Moltmann understanding of Church came from his interpretation of Trinity. As Trinity functions in community which is also pictured in the Jesus' community so is the Church a community of disciple who in the power of Spirit lives the Christ in the world. His ecclesiology developed out of dissatisfaction which he developed as an observer of the present condition of the Church which is akin to the Trinitarian community. On the one hand, traditional Churches with large organization do have programme that care for people but have less hold on the people spiritually. Indifference towards the Church is growing. There is a growing gap witnessed among the clergy-believers' relationship. On the other hand, many new counter movements in the form of numerous independent Churches focuses more on individuals and their participation in the Church. But due to lack of proper administrational set up, has led to the creation of many new Churches without accountability. It might be the modern thrust on self-consciousness that put individual at the top of the hierarchy and brought Churches into the hands of the affluent. For him, Church should be relational and critical. He writes, "The Church cannot understand itself alone. It can only truly comprehend its mission and its meaning, its roles and functions in relation to others."[132] Through this relational project, Moltmann tries to breathe new life into the nature of Church as community without denying its holistic meaning. Church must be a messianic community oriented in mission towards the coming kingdom of God for serving the world which is a critique to the modern Pentecostal movements that hails personal devotion at the expense of the world. The messianic fellowship in the community not only engages visibly in the world but also moves around in a trinitarian fashion in the history and augments its anticipation towards the eschatological fulfillment.[133] The mission of God the Father was carried out by Christ and is continued with the presence of the Spirit through the Church to the eschatological future. The Spirit is working among the members of the Church without any distinction in a friendly way. It is only in friendship that one can enter into a creative relationship. To put it differently in the words of Baukham, Church fulfills its messianic vocation not by absolutizing itself but in open relationship of dialogue and co-operation.[134] Because of the Church relative place in the wider context of the trinitarian history of God, it is 'open for God, open for men and open for the future of both God and men. The Church atrophies when it surrenders any one of this openness and closes itself up against God, men or the future.'[135] This openness tries to heal any sort of exclusive and close nature of community which is reflected in tribal Church.

Will the Church remain the same if it opens itself to other religious faith and communities? How can Church be holy if it compromises itself with the world as the Pentecostals claim? If Church has to impart the kingdom values among the communities then it has to stop claiming and start to give its life for the world because it is for the world that Jesus sacrificed himself. Church cannot exist if it closes and keeps itself away untouched from the world. Church will remain holy only in the life and work of Christ (1 Cori 1:2; 6:11). Holiness means here not a higher sphere of divine power, before which people shudder and shrink back rather it consists of being made holy, in sanctification, the subject of the activity of being God (1 Thess. 5:23; II Thess. 2:13). God sanctifies his Church by calling the godless through Christ, by justifying sinners, and by accepting the lost.[136] The community of saints is therefore always, as Luther believed, the community of sinners. As 1 John 1:8 says, "If we say we have no sin, we deceive ourselves, and the truth is not in us." Church should base itself in the Jesus' historical model of community rather centering only in the Word.

The very acceptance of the guilt by the upper caste people and the change in the attitude of the traditional churches are all part of the sanctification process which can be witnessed in the liberation and the sanctification of nations. Church is not beyond space and time rather it participates in liberating the people in bondage, solidarity with weak and helpless, fellowship of freedom and equality in the Spirit.[137] The real subject of his ecclesiology belong to the 'grassroots' communities of Christians. Therefore, any reform in the Church should start 'from below' communities.[138] The work of the Spirit is not confined to the Church because the Spirit works everywhere in creation. In his words, it is the *community of creation* that recognizes the operation of the life-giving Spirit of God in the trend to relationship in created things.[139] Therefore, the Church cannot absolutize itself, but it is always provisional in nature to minister as steward to the world around us. Therefore, a messianic friendship would bring all the cosmic reality and historical reality in unity and might bridge the gap of transcendental and worldly limitations existing in today's Church.

It has been observed that historical models of Church focused on the one hand the community nature of the Church, on the other hand it worked for its own territorial and religious expansion creating a hierarchical and institutional model by ignoring the Kingdom values. Church became a place where people belonging to similar caste, class and interest flock together for fellowship. Here Moltmann asserts that it is in difference that community discovers its worth as a liberating community just as God in its trinitarian function work together in difference but with unity in the history of the world. If Trinitarian community of Moltmann hinges on the experience of friendship and fellowship of the whole cosmos without any uniformity towards the eschatological fulfillment then the Sarvodaya Church relishes its eschatological fulfillment in the experience of people those who are oppressed and marginalized along with their oppressors in their pilgrimage towards a new horizon where all remain one in Christ.

## Towards a paradigmatic Ecclesiology of *Sarvodaya*

The previous section has provided a categorical reflection on the Church suited for the Indian situation which is marked by various cultural, religious, economic and political orientations. But a critical analysis has exposed the weaknesses inherent in their ecclesiology. The ecclesiology of Moltmann would pave the way for a better proposal in the Indian context. The 'community' aspect of Moltmann might provide convincing elements that would substantiate the ontological as well as functional necessity of the Church in India.

## A Sarvodaya Church

The term *Sarvodaya* means the 'liberation of all.'[140] The meaning of Sarvodaya lies in its nature of taking all the living being together irrespective of any class, caste, gender, sex, species etc. and work for the liberation of all. It is a name that Mahatma Gandhi and his followers gave to a new social order that they sought to establish in India. It is a social idea which aims at the full development of the individual and the greatest good of all. In this Sarvodaya community all the individuals will have equal opportunities for the healthy development of all inherent abilities. The individual will use their fully developed talents for the good of others.[141] It forms the basis of *ahimsa*. In this community, the opponents are not destroyed but converted to be friends through self-suffering and conflicts are resolved.[142] Here Moltmann delivers the same opinion, the community of brethren, is really the fellowship of friends who live in the friendship of Jesus and spread friendliness in the fellowship, by meeting the forsaken with affection and the despised with respect.[143] Sarvodaya neither follows the legacy of traditional Churches in the sense of a formal community guided by the principles of ecclesial set-up under a supreme authority nor it come under the umbrella of modern ecclesiology in rendering full individual preferences and postmodern claim of liberation of the oppressed. Rather, it advocates for the liberation of all, even the oppressors from their oppressing attitude. In the words of Moltmann, it is a cosmological community where all are held in equal terms and experience the liberative praxis of God. Sarvodaya community is a theological reality where God, Humans and other living beings live in perfect relationship. It is a community that critiques any individual or group-based community and deals with it in a holistic way addressing to the issues of each and every life form. In other words, it is a corporeal community. The ecological disaster by Humans for selfish gains destroys the vision of Sarvodaya. Church as a community for all should stand for the cause of whole cosmos and fight for the justice. How can Church as a community of believers in Christ represent a universal community with different nomenclatures? If death, suffering and division were born in the universal community through the disobedience of humans then, Church which lives in Christ who is the epitome of humanity represent the inauguration of the beginning of a new era of universal reconciliation and liberation among the communities through his life, death and resurrection. Church through its vision and mission becomes the foundation in imparting the kingdom values to all communities that are drenched in chaos and thereby becoming the icon of universal liberation. The starting point for all liberation is the protest. Protest is the proper attitude of a community that has been addressed by the word of the other.[144] It means not just an active objection to a situation, but also an act of professing a faith, a fundamental conviction. It is a conviction of community of those who are moved and shaken, but those who also understand. Jan Patocka called this the 'solidarity of the shaken.' He writes, "the solidarity of the shaken; the solidarity of those who are capable of understanding what life and death is all about. That history is the conflict of *mere life*, barren and chained to fear, with *life at its* peak, life that does not plan for the ordinary days of a future but sees clearly that the everyday, its life and its 'peace,' have an end.... The "solidarity of the shaken" is built up in persecution and uncertainty."[145] To phrase it differently, Church as a community is a space of grace and of condemnation, a thread of glory and of shame. It is a place of healing and salvation brought out from the conduit of Spirit. It is a community of those who in the margin barely hanging on to life are sustained unutterable turmoil able to name and be named by their relationship to God and to one another. In short, Church as Sarvodaya community is not only intended to bring liberation through protest to the Dalits, Women and Tribals of India but also celebrating along with the whole cosmos that has been under the yoke of suffering to a renewed life of creativity.

## Church: A Dialogical community

Moltmann affirms that truth is to be found in unhindered dialogue.[146] Community based on Sarvodaya model that tallies on liberation becomes a reality only through dialogue. Here ecclesiology is 'Church-talk.' It is a talk of the Church received from the command of the Lord and addressing to its surroundings. Church with all its veracity has to deal with the issues of Indian context. It can be relevant only in relation to the existing community outside of its four walls. As Pannenberg affirms that the real expression of community life is found outside the Church where the people work or play or live their family life.[147] In other words, Church needs to be dialogical in vocation so as to accept and accommodate the calling and task of other religious communities. India which is a home of many religious traditions should not be viewed by the Church as the arena of devil's workshop but as a potential partner in the history of the world. Moltmann says, "Fruitful dialogue involves clear knowledge about the identity of one's own faith on the one hand; but on the other it requires a feeling of one's own incompleteness and a real sense of need for fellowship with the other."[148] Dialogue can only create a condition for fellowship in which mutual participation, exchange and cross-fertilization become possible. Church will never be a liberating icon if it is embedded in the narrow supra-spirituality of individualism or traditionalism. If Church is a redeeming agent from the evils of the world then the Church herself should be redeemed from the *bhakti* of their absolute truth claims. As dialogue is an inevitable part of human existence so is the Church a model of dialogue for human spiritual sustenance. Dialogue is possible only when Church receives its vocation as God's agent in preparing the platform for bringing different religious tradition together. In this dialogue, there is not only the sharing of ideas but also understanding and participating in each other faith. To put it differently, dialogue is not just a verbal expression but an ongoing event where the hearts of the participants are converted. It is turning towards the other with an open heart. Paulos Mar Gregorios says that in dialogue one party takes the initiative to seek out the other, "realizing the other in his particular existence, even the encompassing of him, so that the situation common to him and oneself are experienced also from his, the other's end."[149] Here the differences are witnessed and celebrated with no inherent discrepancies mutating and influencing from the backyard of Church totalitarian politics. Dialogue cannot be subsumed into communicative model but has to bear the otherness of the other and enter into the depth of the understanding of God. It is only through God's love that one can able to discover the value of life in one's community and in the world. It is the ongoing situation of the world that makes the dialogue inevitable. The issues of fundamentalism, oppression of Dalits and women in the name of caste and gender respectively should be the highlight of any dialogue. Church through dialogue should deal with the issue of regionalism where people belonging to a particular region consider themselves as superior to other regions in terms of education, economy and culture.

Dialogue should not be limited to the world of humans, but it should penetrate into the cosmic sphere. In the context of ecological disaster, Church should involve in continuous dialogue with nature, the creation of God, so as to save the world from destruction. The kind of human relationship to nature which has created the ecological crisis and must be superseded is that of exploitative domination. As God has created human in his image and likeness so is the entire cosmos the mirror of God's trinitarian relationship. Destroying nature will bring a destruction in God self because God and his creation are indispensable part of each other. Therefore, Church in India should become a community that live as partner in the liberation of the whole creation for the reign of messianic Kingdom.

## Church as *'Kindom'* of God- An 'other' Community

The concept of the Kingdom of God is very vibrant in many theological writings. In the pluralistic context of India Church understands itself as the 'sign and sacrament of the Kingdom of God.' Church has ideally been regarded as the Kingdom of God. But today it is accepted that the Kingdom inaugurated by Christ and the Church cannot be identified. The very purpose of the Church which is to stand for the liberation of the people has mandated for the cause of the influential. Although the reality of the Kingdom is present within the Church, the Kingdom cannot be exclusively contained within the Church. It is a larger reality where people are converted to the unconditional love towards neighbour and to God. This love is reflected in the acceptance of an inclusive community where prophetic spirituality is practiced through its care for the weak, the marginal, the poor and the orphans. Jesus' preaching and teaching of the Kingdom of God was exactly an alternative to the Temple community and advocated a non-authoritative, non-hierarchical, non-exploitative and an egalitarian community based on sharing and service.[150] In short, Jesus inaugurated an 'other' community.

But the term 'Kingdom' itself reflect an authoritative domain that rules over its subject for its own stability. Therefore, the word *'Kindom'* is suitable because of its characteristic nature of accepting every individual as equal in the community of relationship that entails a mutual love in Christ. *Kindom* of God is a subversive concept that charges against the forces of oppression and stands for the cause of justice. In this Kindom there are no more strangers, rather they are related to one another and they stand for the cause of one another. It is an 'other' community that is been freed from the clutches of elite and influential in the community and walk in the pathway to freedom. This freedom is the fulfillment of the promises of God through Christ. As Moltmann says, "The gospel calls men and women out of the bondage of sin, law and death and puts them on the road to righteousness and the freedom of eternal life."[151] This is possible only in the power of the Spirit because the Spirit of God is the creator of new future and the new creator of what is transient for this future. Therefore, in the Kindom of God, Spirit governs the life of the people for a new future where there would be no struggles and war in the name of caste, class, gender, region and religion. Thus, a relevant Church in India would look forward in the building of a Kindom community for a meaningful existence in the world.

## Church as a *Kuttukettu* Community

The nature of the Church should not be restricted to Kindom values, but it should cater the virtue of friendship. The term *Kuttukettu* is a Malayalam word for friendship which encompasses a myriad set of virtues that exist in the relationship between individuals. Moltmann's concept of friendship model is a stepping stone in emulating a better notion of Church in Indian situation. In the Indian scenario which is marked by multi-cultural, multi-religious, multilingual and multi-regional, Church needs to be an experience that embraces the quality of friend in relation to others in the society. A friend is necessarily not a person emerged out of blood relation, rather it is born out of the womb of relationship. Friendship should not fall into the trench of exclusivity as that of Greek community which was based on reciprocity or parity principle.[152] Friendship can be maintained among the people belonging to similar background but in order to understand the beauty of friendship, it is necessary to relate with the people of other communities, region and religion. In the language of Felix Wilfred, it is by crossing the borders that one might engage a critical and creational relationship. Church cannot always represent itself as an institution guarding the interest of the Church but as a true friend giving a hand of solidarity and affection in the time of need. Friendship should also not be a vocation of private affairs secluded from public domain. Rather it should emulate the friendship of Jesus that goes beyond the private affairs to the public protection of and public respect for others. The effect of this friendship transforms the hostile world into a pleasant world. It brings to light a harmony with other men and women, with God, and with creation, and overcomes discord by accepting the forsaken. It is only by experiencing the friendship in this way that a *kindom* community can be realized.

## Community of *Park* fellowship

In India various places are used for fellowship especially in religious, social or cultural institutions. The social places like clubs and recreation centers etc., provide spaces for the people to discuss various matters. One of such places is the *Park*. It is a fellowship where different people belonging to different background come together either for a walk or for a conscious gathering to discuss various matters. It is very informal gathering which is not intended to share gospel in a traditional way rather through understanding and accepting each other, a friendly platform is created. This platform would provide the way for sharing the love of Christ. The informal setting of these groups can enable the gathered community to come out of its so-called religious temper and give space for discussing day to day life situation and search for answers. This would strengthen the relations with the people of other faiths in a friendly and productive manner and also enable the emergence of a new order connected in love. This Park fellowship is different from Chenchiah's *veranda* fellowship because of the nature of being in a public place for all kinds of people whereas in veranda fellowship only intellectuals are gathered for a conscious debates and discussions.

## A Festive Community

The multi-religious context of India is enriched with many festivals owing to its religious demands or as a remembrance of any historical figures. Religious feasts have always shown the meaning of the regeneration of life from its eternal origin. The festivals are the occasion for the people to gather together and celebrate. Feasts are arranged and enjoyed. It provides a sense of unity in the community and reminds the people of their responsibility in sustaining the effectiveness of the community. Here all the difference whether rich or poor; healthy or weak; religious or non-religious etc. are gathered with one heart i.e. to enjoy life to its fullest extent. In other words, the feast widens the traditionally fixed elements of the celebration in order to allow for spontaneous and creative contributions. In the Christian festivity like Easter, hymns, plays and dance are performed as a celebration of the victory of Life. It corresponds to the liberation experienced in the presence of the risen Christ. To put it differently, it is the festal liberation of life. If the incarnation, resurrection and the cross stands at the center of resistance to the existing domination, slavery, discrimination and injustices then the people of India especially the Dalits, Tribal and women stand as the chief guest in the carnival of life. Throughout the criticism of evil, the feast will be an affirmation of existence and thus also an expression of joy in that existence.

## Story-telling Community

The fellowship which corresponds to the gospel in its original interpretation is the messianic community. It is a fellowship which narrates the story of Christ, and its own story with the story of Christ, because its own existence, fellowship and activity spring from the story of liberation. It is a story-telling community, by virtue of its remembrance of the story of Christ and its hope for the *kindom* of human, liberates men and women from the compulsive actions of existing societies. It frees them for a life designed by the messianic character. This story telling was the very fabric of Indian cultural ethos, particularly the dalits and tribals, which was made irrelevant in the whirlwind of Brahmanism and modernization. This story telling connects the people together as community and gives their identity. Story-telling becomes liberative when it is exercised in the community. Church as a community needs to rejuvenate the tradition of the story-telling and fight for the cause of those people whose identity has been jeopardized under the banner of class, caste, gender and sex.

## Conclusion

The self-understanding of the Church today has been analyzed and understood in the light of the self-understanding of the Church at its origins as the Jesus community, and how the notion of community has undergone various nuances in various periods of the Church's history. Church being a divine-human reality is an agent of human salvation. However, the visible structures, doctrines and beliefs, rituals, ministries and its particular understandings of mission are the product of history, though shaped by the Spirit of Jesus are not without distortion and failures of human elements. In the Indian socio-economic and religio-cultural context, the Church is faced with several challenges to which Church has to respond creatively by evolving new ways of being and becoming the Church. Christ centered ecclesiology can become a stumbling block for a dialogical community in a multi-religious context. The Indian models of Church that oriented itself from a Brahmanical framework were counteracted by different subaltern movements that based themselves on equality and justice with an exclusive methodology. Church needs to resuscitate the lost flavour and fervor of community that would take into account the subaltern groups and other communities in the spirit of friendship for the liberation of all. It is a trinitarian friendship that draws upon the love of God through the sacrificial death of Jesus in history and in communion with the Spirit towards an eschatological friendly future.

## Endnotes

[1] Bhagwan Das, "Dalits and the Caste System" in *Indigenous People: Dalits,* edited by James Massey (Delhi: ISPCK, 1994), 58.

[2] Felix Wilfred, "Subaltern and Ethical Auditing," *Jeevadhara* Vol. XXXVII/ No. 217 (January 2007): 7.

[3] S.M. Michael, "Cultural Studies and Theologizing on the Empowerment of Dalits in India" in *Frontiers in Dalit Hermeneutics*, edited by James Massey and Samson Prabhakar (Bangalore: BTESSC/SATHRI, 2005), 71. Also refer Jimmy Dabhi, "Dalit Human Rights: Issues and Perspectives," *Social Action* Vol. 24/No. 1 (Jan-March 2004): 34, 36;

[4] Refer Sukhadeo Thorat Committee Report: Caste Discrimination in AIIMS," *Economic and Political Weekly* Vol. XLII/ No. 22 (June 2-8, 2007): 2032.

[5] S. Anand, "Lighting Out for the Territory: The Arduous Journey of Modern Dalit Literature" in *Caravan*, Vol. 3 No. 2, February 2011, 64-75.

[6] Corinne Scott, "The Context for Feminist Theologizing: Violence Against Women/ Women Against Violence" in *Feminist Theology: Perspectives*

*and Praxis* edited by Prasanna Kumari (Chennai: Gurukul Lutheran Theological College and Research Instute, 1999), 331-338. Also refer Moumita Biswas and Janejinda Pawadee, "Gender Justice in the Grassroots," in *CCA News*, Vol.45 No.1, March 2010, 16.

[7] Gabriele Dietrich and Bas Wielenga, *Towards Understanding Indian Society* (Madurai: Tamilnadu Theological Seminary, 1997), 37.

[8] "Krishna Iyer Demands Probe into Charges against Chief Justices," Kochi Correspondent, *Indian Express*, Wednesday, September 22, 2010, 5.

[9] Ibid., 145, 176.

[10] Purnima S. Tripathi, "Offence as Defense" in *Frontline*, Vol. 28 No. 3, February 11, 2011, 112.

[11] John Desroachers, *Towards a New India* (Bangalore: CSA, 1995), 91.

[12] Lancy Lobo, "Communalism and Christian Response in India" in *Vidyajyoti Journal of Theological Reflection* Vol. LIX/ No.6 (June 1995): 367. Also refer Vidya Subramaniam and J. Venkatesan, "The winding paths of a Temple town," in *The Hindu*, Wednesday, Sept 22, 2010, 12.

[13] Venkitesh Ramakrishnan, "Swami's Confession," in *Frontline* Vol. 28 No. 3, February 11, 2011, 107; Also refer Madhavi Tata, "A Nephew's Tale" in *Outlook* Vol. 51 No. 4, January 2011, 12; "Hindu Terrorism" in *Dalit Voice*, Vol. 30 No. 5, March 2011, 12.

[14] T.A. John, "Gender Equality: Chasing a Millennium Goal for the Long Haul," *Social Action* Vol. 57/ No. 2 (April- June 2007):161-162.

[15] "India fast becoming Superpower," in *Indian Express*, Wednesday, September 22, 2010, 1.

[16] Dietrich and Wielenga, *Towards Understanding Indian Society*, 112.

[17] Ibid., 114.

[18] Simon Paul D'souza, "India at Sixty" in *Integral Liberation* Vol. 2/No. 3 (September 2007): 176-178. Also refer Santhosh Desai, "Constructing Brand India" in *Seminar 618*, February 2011, 14-17.

[19] Y. Moses, "Peoples' Politics and the role of Indian Church," *NCC Review* Vol. CXXVI/ No. 10 (Nov 2006): 50.

[20] Sarah Hiddleston, "Poisoned" in *Frontline*, Sept. 24, 2010, 4 -21.

[21] James David, "Special Economic Zones," in *Integral Liberation* Vol. 2/ No. 3 (September 2007):185-189.

[22] Desrochers, *Towards a New India*, 113-114.

[23] Lancy Lobo, "Injustices to Staines' Memory" in *Indian Currents*, Vol. 23 No. 6, January 2011, 36.

[24]Ashgar Ali Engineer, "2010-Year of Communal Riots," in *Indian Currents,* Vol. 23 No.2, December 2010, 11-13.

[25] A.S. Hemrom, "The Role of Churches in building up Adivasi Solidarity: The Call for an Ecumenical Task," *NCC Review* Vol. CXXX/No. 2 (February 2004): 65. Also refer Ram Puniyani, "Common Minimum Program and Outcome of Secularism" *Social Action* Vol. LIV/No.3 (July-September 2006), 291.

[26] M.G. Radha Krishnan, "Ire of the Minorities," *India Today* Vol. XXXIII/No.1 (Jan 1-7, 2008): 21.

[27] N.B. Mitra, "Bishops Condemn Government Assault on Minority Rights," *People's Reporter* Vol. 20/ No. 3 (Feb 10-25, 2007): 3.

[28] K.L. Schmidt, "Ekklesia," *Theological Dictionary of the New Testament,* edited by Gerhard Kittel, translated by Geoffrey Bromiley Vol. 3 (Michigan: Eerdmans Publishing Company, 1965, Reprint 1976), 504.

[29] Ibid., 516.

[30] *Edhah* is usually translated as synagogue. After exile this became the regular term for Sabbath day meeting of Jews for prayer and study of torah. Thus, it had use for the building in which the meeting took place. This may be the factor for the primitive Chirstian community that took *qahal* for *ekklesia.* See further Edmund Hill, "Church" in *The New Dictionary of Theology,* eds. Joseph A. Komonchak, Mary Collins and Dermot A. Lane (Bangalore: Theological Publication of India, 1996), 185-186.

[31] Schmidt, "Ekklesia," 515.

[32] George M. Soares-Prabhu, "Radical Beginnings: The Jesus Community as the Archetype of the Church," *Jeevadhara,* Vol. XV, No. 88 (1985), 310-318. See, Gerd Theissen, *The First Followers of Jesus* (London: SCM Press, 1978).

[33] James P. Martin, "The Church in Mathew," in *Interpreting the Gospels,* edited by James Luther Mays (Philadelphia: Fortress Press, 1981), 97- 114.

[34] Wolfhart Pannenberg, *Systematic Theology* Vol. 3, translated by Geoffrey W. Bromiley (Michigan: William Eerdmans Publishing Company, 1998), 29.

[35] Kuncheria Pathil, *Theology of the Church New Horizon* (Bangalore: Dharmaram Publications, 2006), 57.

[36] Refer to the section of Moltmann's messianic community in chapter two.

[37] G.S.M Walker, "Church," *New Bible Dictionary,* 2nd edition (Secunderabad: Operation Mobilization, 1990, reprint 1993), 205.

38 Schmidt, "Ekklesia," 506.

39 Ibid., 507.

40 Raymond E. Brown, *The Churches: The Apostles Left Behind* (New York: Paulist Press, 1984), 34.

41 Eric G. Jay, *The Church: Its Changing Image through Twenty Centuries*, Vol., *The First Sixteen Centuries* (London: SPCK, 1977), 112.

42 Paul Tillich, *A Complete History of Christian Thought* edited by Carl E. Braaten (New York: Harper and Row Publishers, 1968), 33-50.

43 Jacques Dupuis and Neuner eds., *The Christian Faith* (Bangalore: Theological Publication of India, 1978), 265.

44 Richard P. Mcbrien, "Church," in *A New Dictionary of Christian Theology*, edited by Alan Richardson and John Bowden (London: SCM Press Ltd, 1983), 109.

45 Tony Lane, *The Lion Book of Christian Thought* (Tiruvalla: Suvartha Bhavan, 1999), 32.

46 Wilbert Kreiss, *History of the Reformation*, translated by Theodore Mueller (USA: LCMS, 1998), 9.

47 John H. Leith, "Ecclesiology," in *A Handbook of Christian Theology*, edited by Donald W. Musser and Joseph L. Prince (Nashville: Abingdon Press, 1992), 136.

48 J.N.D. Kelly, *Early Christian Doctrines* (New York: Harpers Collins Publishers, 1978), 189.

49 Tillich, *A Complete History of Christian Thought*, 40.

50 Between 500-1500 C.E.

51 O.J. Thatcher and E.H. Mc Neal, *A Source Book for Medieval History* (New York: Harper and Row Publishers, 1905), 136-138.

52 Kreiss, *History of the Reformation*, 8.

53 Ruth Rouse, *A History of the Ecumenical Movement 1517-1948*, edited by Stephen Neil (Geneva: WCC, 1989), 27.

54 William R. Estep, *Renaissance and Reformation* (Michigan: William Eerdmans Publishing Company, 1986), 1-6.

55 Georgia Harkness, *Mysticism: Its Meaning and Message* (Nashville: Abingdon Press, 1953), 17.

56 Justo L. Gonzalez, *A History of Christian Thought*, Vol. 3 (Nashville: Abingdon Press, 1975), 15-16.

57 Williston Walker. *A History of the Christian Church*, 4th edition (Edinburgh: T&T Clark Ltd., 1986), 320.

[58] F.L. Cross ed., *The Oxford Dictionary of the Christian Church* (New York: Oxford University Press, 1957. reprint 1961), 1069.

[59] Hans Schwarz, *The Christian Church* (Minneapolis: Augsburg: Publishing House, 1982), 157.

[60] M. Rebeiro, "Origin of the Church," in *Living Word* 3/13 (May-June 1989):141.

[61] Karkkainen, *An Introduction to Ecclesiology*, 39.

[62] Martin Luther, "On the Councils and the Churches," translated by C.M. Jacobs in *Works of Martin Luther* with Introduction and notes, Vol. V (Philadelphia: Muhlenberg Press, 1931), 265.

[63] Estep, *Renaissance and Reformation*, 157.

[64] It is sociological reference to community living in urban areas where the community lives their relationship based on contract which means if a person provides services to another then the latter should some favour in return.

[65] McBrien, "Church," 110.

[66] Karkkainen, *An Introduction to Ecclesiology...*, 28

[67] Karl Rahner, "Observations of the Factor of the Charismatic in the Church," in *Theological Investigations XII* (New York: Seabury, 1974), 97.

[68] That they may be one.

[69] Karkkainen, *An Introduction to Ecclesiology...*, 37.

[70] John Fuellenbach, *Church: Community for the Kingdom* (Maryknoll: Orbis Books, 2002), 152.

[71] Ibid.

[72]. Yves Cogar, *Lay People in the Church: A Study for a Theology of Laity,* (Westminster, MD: Newman, 1965), 28-58.

[73] Kallistos Ware, *The Orthodox Church,* revised edition (London: Penguin, 1993), 240.

[74] Nicholas A. Jesson, *Orthodox Contribution to Ecumenical Ecclesiology* (Toronto: University of St. Michael's College, 2001), 9.

[75] Kallistos Ware, *The Orthodox Way* (New York: St. Vladimir's Seminary Press, 1999), 39.

[76] Ware, *Orthodox...*, 240.

[77] Paulos Mar Gregorios, *A Human God* (Kottayam: Mar Gregorios Foundation, 1992), 30.

[78] The previous section of reformation model before modernity showcased the non-institutional nature of Church that is purely based on the Word of God from the ordained priests. This section would deal with the modern understanding where all believers are given the equal privileges in rendering God's service through the Word of God.

[79] Yves Conger, *I Believe in the Holy Spirit* (New York: Crossroad Herder, 1997), 1:139-140.

[80] Karkkainen, Op.cit., 40.

[81] Eric W. Gritsch and Robert W. Jenson, *Lutheranism: The Theological Movement and its Confessional Writings* (Philadelphia: Fortress Press, 1976), 130-131.

[82] Paul Althaus, *The Theology of Martin Luther*, trans. Robert C. Schultz (Philadelphia: Fortress Press, 1966), 313-318. See also, Pannenberg, *Systematic Theology*, 3: 373.

[83] Vitor Westhelle, *The Church Event*, 104.

[84] The researcher has taken both in similar framework as they give priority to the charismata. It portrays a charismata-based community.

[85] Karkkainen, *An Introduction to Ecclesiology*, 73.

[86] Ibid., 75.

[87] Leslie Newbigin, *The Household of God: Lectures on the Nature of the Church* (London: SCM press, 1953), 106.

[88] W.A. Visser 't Hooft, "The Basis: Its History and Significance," in *Ecumenical Review* 2(1985):86.

[89] This was supported by the WCC, third assembly at New Delhi 1961. Karkkainen, *An Introduction...*, 80.

[90] George Vandervelde, "Koinonia Ecclesiology: Ecumenical Breakthrough," in *One in Christ* 29 (1993): 133.

[91] Carl E. Braaten and Robert W. Jenson ed., "The Church as Communion" in *The Catholicity of Reformation* (Grand Rapids: Eerdmans Publishing Company, 1996), 1-12.

[92] Michael Lawler and Thomas J. Shanahan, *Church: A Spiritual Communion* (Collegeville, Minnesota: Liturgical Press, 1995), 8-11.

[93] Jurgen Moltmann, *The Open Church: An Invitation to a Messianic Lifestyle* (London: SCM Press, 1978), 84.

[94] Paul Varghese, *The Church in India: Where We Headed* (An Unpublished article dated 24.8.1973), 8.

[95] Letty Russell, *Church in the Round: Feminist Interpretation of the Church* (Louisville: Westminster John Knox, 1993), 42.

[96] Ibid., 18.

[97] Ibid., 22-23.

[98] Elizabeth Schussler Fiorenza, *In Memory of Her: A Feminist Reconstruction of Christian Origins* (New York: Crossroad, 1984), 154.

[99] Elizabeth Schussler Fiorenza, *Discipleship of Equals: Critical Feminist Ecclesiology for Liberation* (New York: Crossroad, 1993), 269-274.

[100] Robin Boyd, *An Introduction to Indian Christian Theology* (Delhi: ISPCK, 2000), 159.

[101] Christianity exchanged the living Christ for an elaborate ceremonial institution, for a book, the Bible. He says that as Christianity developed, Church also slowly developed its structure on tradition or on the Bible and its social and religious principles of Roman society. For him, Christianity is a failure because we made a new religion instead of a new creation. P. Chenchiah, "The Living Church or Religious Institution," in *Theology of Chenchiah*, edited by D.A. Thangasamy (Madras: CLS, 1966), 134.

[102] P. Chenchiah, "Kingdom of God, Church and Ashrams," in *Ashrams Past and Present* (Madras: CLS, 1941; reprint, 1996), 276.

[103] Ibid., 278.

[104] Ibid., 276.

[105] Chenchiah, *Rethinking Christianity in India,* ed., D.M Devasahayam and A.N. Sudarisanam, (Madras: Hogarth Press, 1939), 190.

[106] Kappen, *Jesus and Society* (Delhi: ISPCK, 2002), 125.

[107] Ibid., 123.

[108] Sebastian Kappen, *Jesus and Cultural Revolution: An Asian Perspective* (Bombay: Build Publications, 1983), 17.

[109] Ibid.

[110] Ibid., 73.

[111] Sebastian Kappen, *Jesus and Freedom* (Mary knoll: Orbis, 1977), 150.

[112] Ibid., 151.

[113] Refer section 2.4.1.3 of the second chapter.

[114] M.M. Thomas, "The Struggle for Human Dignity as a Preparation for the Gospel" *Renewal for Mission,*

edited by Lyon and Manuel (Madras: CLS, 1976), 101.

115 M.M. Thomas, *The Gospel of Forgiveness and Koinonia* (Delhi: ISPCK and Thiruvalla: CSS, 1994), 44.

116 M.M. Thomas, *Salvation and Humanization: Some Crucial Issues of the Theology of Mission in Contemporary India* (Madras: CLS, 1971), 70.

117 M.M. Thomas, *Towards a Theology of Contemporary Ecumenism* (Madras: CLS, 1970), 139.

118 M.M. Thomas, "Christ-centered Syncretism" in *Religion and Society*, December 21, 1974, 66.

119 Thomas, *Salvation and Humanization*, 4.

120 M.M. Thomas, *Some Theological Dialogues* (Madras: CLS, 1977), 128.

121 Refer to section 2.4.1.6 of second chapter.

122 M.M. Thomas, *Risking Christ for Christ's Sake: Towards an Ecumenical Theology of Pluralism* (Geneva: WCC, Publications, 1987), 3.

123 Abraham Stephen, "Christ and Culture: An Examination of M.M. Thomas' Theology of Religions" in *Contextualization: A Re-reading of M.M. Thomas* edited by Godwin Shiri (Tiruvalla: Christava Sahitya Samithi, 2007), 102.

124 M.M. Thomas, Newbigin, "Salvation and Humanization: A Discussion" in *Mission Trends*, No.1, 1974, 217.

125 James Massey, *Down Trodden: The Struggles of India's Dalits For Identity, Solidarity and Liberation* (Geneva: WCC Publications, 1997), 75.

126 M. Amaladoss, "Mission as Prophesy," in *New Directions in Mission and Evangelization* 2, edited by J.A. Scherer and S.B. Bevans (New York: Orbis, 1994), 68.

127 L. Stanislaus, *The Liberative Mission of the Church among Dalit Christians* (Delhi: ISPCK, 1999), 358.

128 Jurgen Moltmann, *The Future of Creation*, translated by Margaret Kohl (London: SCM Press, 1979), 53-54.

129 K. Thanzauva, *Theology of Community: Tribal Theology in the Making* (Aizwal: Academy of Integrated Christian Studies, 2004), 172.

130 Paulus Kullu, "Tribal Spirituality: An Integrated Life with Belief," *Sevartham* 21(1996): 109.

131 Ibid., 174.

132 Jurgen Moltmann, *Church in the Power of the Spirit*, 13.

133 Ibid., 197-198.

134 Richard Baukham, *The Theology of Jurgen Moltmann* (Edinburgh: T&T Clark, 1995), 126.

[135] Moltmann, *Church in the Power of the Spirit*, 2.

[136] Ibid., 353.

[137] Ibid., 105.

[138] Ibid., 275.

[139] Jurgen Moltmann, *The Spirit of Life: A Universal Affirmation*, trans. Margaret Kohl (Minneapolis: Fortress Press, 1992; reprint, 1993), 225.

[140] It was first used by Acharya Samantbhadra, a Jain servant of 2nd century A.D. It was later taken by Gandhiji along with his influence from John Ruskin's "Unto the last' to explain his action, in his liberative freedom movement of India.

[141] Daniel Mangaleth, *A Challenge and A Promise: Mahatma Gandhi's Philosophy of Life*

(Trivandrum: M S Publications, 1996), 104.

[142] Ibid. Also refer P. Nagaraja Rao, *Mahatma Gandhi: Centenary Lectures* (Delhi: Everest Press, 1972), 77-79.

[143] Moltmann, *Church in the Power of the Spirit*, 316.

[144] Jan Patocka, *Heretical Essay in the Philosophy of History* (Chicago: Open Court, 1996), p. 134. Also refer, Vitor Westhelle, *The Church Event*, 103.

[145] Ibid., 105.

[146] Moltmann, "Preface," *The Trinity and the Kingdom...*, xiii.

[147] Wolfhart Pannenberg, *The Church*, translated by Keith Crim (Philadelphia: Westminster Press, 1983), 17.

[148] Moltmann, *The Church in the Power...*, 159.

[149] Paulos Mar Gregorios, *Inter Church Dialogue* (Delhi: ISPCK/MGF, 2010), 3.

[150] Joseph G. Aryankalayil, "The Biblical Concept of the Kingdom of God and the Historical Reality of the Church" in *Journal of Sacred Scriptures* Vol. 5 No. Jan 2011, 19-43.

[151] Moltmann, *Church in the Power of the Spirit*, 191.

[152] Moltmann, *The Open Church*, 60-61.

# Conclusion

The author has made an attempt in this book to emphasize the theological relevance of the concept of "Community" and draw the holistic picture of community for constructing an ecclesiology suited for Indian context. Community has been the hallmark of all cultures. It has brought the life and identity of the people in the culture to a more meaningful experience of their existence and unabatedly adds participation among the members of community in the building of a just community. Today, it has been observed that the organic nature which is characteristics of Indian community is taking a shift caricatured by rising modernization, religious fundamentalism, globalization, communal politics, individualism and parochialism. Due to Urbanization, communities based on filial and emotional relationship is overrun by end-based relations. Community is being driven away from the emotional side to a commercial face of human existence characterized by capitalism and individualism. As Religion plays a major role in the formation and sustenance of community has been interpenetrated by selfish political motives. Communities are created for ascertaining power over other communities by inciting the religious sentiments of the people. The Sangh Pariwar of the Hindutva movement is the prime example of how they use power to control Christian community. Communalized politics are playing a big role in jettisoning the essential function of community.

Researcher argues that this shift of community values is not alien to Christianity as Church which was born as a community in the model of Jesus' movement has been ransacked by the thieves of Christian autocracy. Jesus modeled his community based on friendship and fellowship which was followed by the first century Christians. Later this was shifted to a more hierarchical and power centered society. The community values inherent in the Church were met with plethora of reform movements leading to various denominations that brought the community of Jesus to the background. As a responsible community, the Church is called to witness Christ by participating in the struggles of the people for the restoration of human dignity.

Researcher has analyzed carefully different ecclesiological model, both Western and Indian, with its thrust on community pattern. Though early Christianity followed the pattern of Jesus' community model united in the love of Jesus Christ but was overridden with an administrative and hierarchical setup. Under the leadership of bishops and Papacy, Church got an institutionalized form and was used to acquire political power and authority. As a result, Church lost its community values, its vibrancy and freedom. However, from the early period of institutionalism it had to confront a number of protest movements. Reformation brought a big breakthrough in the understanding and purpose of the Church as a community in the world. Luther's teachings such as 'justification by faith alone,' 'priesthood of all believers' etc. challenged the spiritual tyranny of the Church and Papal authority thereby bringing the community of Christ under God's word. Church became too 'Word' centered that it forgot its mission as salt and light to the world. Instead of becoming *for* the world, it became an entity *in* the world. Instead of becoming a *space* for the world it started to *create* spaces among itself. All the constructive ecclesiology created their own spaces to avenge the dominant spaces rather than being a community of all equals.

The community understanding of different Indian ecclesiology, particularly P. Chenchiah, Sebastian Kappen and M.M. Thomas provided some path breaking insights where the importance of community is held high. Chenchiah brought the *Ashrama* model to represent the community concept of the Church which escapes the holistic nature of Indian ethos. Sebastian Kappen unfolds the nature of community from the perspective of discipleship that pertains to the service of humanity, but it misses the transcendental nature of Christian spirituality. M.M. Thomas took the importance of community seriously and suggested a Christ-centered humanity with pluralism as its wheels. The humanized community founded in Christ strengthens the nation through participation and the well-being of all. But again, his Christ centeredness appears to represent a form of cultural chauvinism which might not lead to a holistic formation of community. In short, the Indian theologians tried to rejuvenate the concept of community from the perspective of the demands posed by the society.

However, the researcher would like to draw some insights from Jurgen Moltmann who has spent a substantial amount of time in travelling across third world countries and tried to sketch a form of community that would gratify the need of the Church in the Indian scenario. His understanding of messianic fellowship overrides any kind of boundary whether it is caste, class or gender. The space, for him, is the notion of friendship. For him, a community needs to be related to each other based on functional aspect, but it should ontologically knit together with the thread of selfless friendship and fellowship. Church can fill the spaces created by autocracy, hierarchy, individualism, parochialism and modernization etc. only when it has the daring to be open and invite humanity to live for a common cause. But the question Moltmann faces was how we can dream of a common humanity in the multi-religious context? He decisively opines that it is under the cross of Christ that the community finds the true fellowship. Does it also not show Christ centeredness? He argues that the cross of Christ is not icon or a material to be followed blindly rather it is an event where love was released selflessly through Christ's sacrifice. It is this love that forms the umbrella of the cross and which can be witnessed only in a true friendship. A true friend will always be ready to dialogue and try to free away any sort of prejudices intrinsic to it. Church as a community based on friendship will always stand for the cause of marginalized and oppressed irrespective of any social and cultural classification.

For the researcher, a Church should be a *Sarvodaya* community that dreams for the 'rise of all.' A Sarvodaya community not only makes a person feel secure and friendly but it rises itself on the stand of divine imperative to protest against all the injustices, corruption, violence and prejudices prowling in the Indian context. It is a dialogical community that stands under the cross of Christ and mediates for a world where love and pain are united in our common cause for a Kindom world. The community fulfills the task of a midwife who patiently helps and mediates the world to receive the unfathomable love and pain poured out on us by God through his only son. And when received the moment is celebrated leaving behind all differences that had left separated for the past thousands of years. To quote from Walter Benjamin, "If the theory is correct that feeling is not located in the head, that we sentimentally experience a window, a cloud, a tree not in our brains but, rather, in the place where we see it, then we are, in looking at our beloved, too, outside ourselves. But in a torment of tension and ravishment. Out feeling dazzled, flutters like a flock of birds.... And as the birds seek refuge in the leafy recesses of a tree...feeling escape into...where they can lie low in safety. And no passer-by would guess that it is just here, in what is defective and censurable, that the fleeting darts of adoration nestle."[1]

## Endnote

[1] Walter Benjamin, Reflections: Essays, Aphorisms, Autobiographical Writings (New York: Schocken, 1986), 68.

# Bibliography

## Primary Sources

Moltmann, Jurgen. *The Way of Jesus Christ: Christology in Messianic Dimension.* London: SCM, 1990.

_____. *A Broad Place: An Autobiography,* trans. by Margaret Kohl. Minneapolis, U.S.A: Fortress Press. 2008.

_____. "Autobiographical Note" in A.J. Conyers, *God, Hope and History: Jurgen Moltmann and the Christian Concept of History.* Macon, Ga.: Mercer University Press, 1988.

_____. *Experience of God.* Philadelphia: Fortress Press, 1980.

_____. *The Way of Jesus Christ: Christology in Messianic Dimension,* translated by Margaret Kohl. San Francisco: Harper and Row, 1990.

_____. *Trinity and the Kingdom of God.* New York: Harper Collins, 1981.

_____. *God in Creation: An Ecological Doctrine of Creation.* Trans. Margaret Kohl. London: SCM Press, 1985.

_____. *History and the Triune God.* New York: Crossroad, 1991.

_____. *The Church in the Power of the Holy Spirit.* London: SCM Press, 1977.

_____. *The Open Church: An Invitation to a Messianic Lifestyle.* London: SCM Press, 1978.

_____. *The Crucified God: The Cross as the Foundation and Criticism of Christian Theology.* London: SCM Press, 1974.

_____. *God for a Secular Society: The Public Relevance of Theology.* Minneapolis: Fortress Press, 1999.

_____. *The Spirit of Life: A Universal Affirmation,* trans. Margaret Kohl. Minneapolis: Fortress Press, 1992; reprint, 1993.

_____. "Pentecost and the Theology of Life," *Concillium* 03 (1996).

# Secondary Sources

## Books, Dictionaries and Encyclopedias

Althaus, Paul. *The Theology of Martin Luther*. Translated by Robert C. Schultz. Philadelphia: Fortress Press, 1966.

Amaladoss, M. "Mission as Prophesy," in *New Directions in Mission and Evangelization* 2. Edited by J.A. Scherer and S.B. Bevans. New York: Orbis, 1994.

Anderson, B. *Imagined Communities: Reflections on the Origin and Spread of Nationalism*. London: Verso, 1983.

Anderson, Bernard W. *Contours of Old Testament Theology*. Minneapolis: Fortress Press, 1999.

Aristotle, *Metaphysics* bilingual ed.; trans. Hugh Tredennick. Cambridge: Harvard University Press, 1933.

Ayoub, Mahmoud. *Islam: Faith and History*. England: One World Publications, 2006.

Baukham, Richard. *The Theology of Jurgen Moltmann*. Edinburgh: T&T Clark, 1995.

_____. "Jurgen Moltmann," in *The Modern Theologians*, ed. David F. Ford. Oxford: Blackwell Publishers, 1989.

Benjamin, Walter. *Reflections: Essays, Aphorisms, Autobiographical Writings* New York: Schocken, 1986.

Bonhoeffer, Dietrich. *No Rusty Swords*. New York: Harper and Row, 1965.

Boyd, Robin. *An Introduction to Indian Christian Theology*. Delhi: ISPCK, 2000.

Braaten Carl E. and Robert W. Jenson ed. "The Church as Communion" in *The Catholicity of Reformation*. Grand Rapids: Eerdmans Publishing Company, 1996.

Brown, Raymond E. *The Churches: The Apostles Left Behind*. New York: Paulist Press, 1984.

Caplan, Lionel. "From 'Community' to 'communities' in the Indian Church? in *Culture, Religion and Society: Essays in honour of Richard W. Taylor*. Edited by S.K. Chaterjee and H.P. Mabry. Delhi: ISPCK, 1996.

Chettimattam, John B. *Patterns of Indian Thought*. Mary knoll: Orbis, 1971.

Chenchiah, P. "The Living Church or Religious Institution," in *Theology of Chenchiah*. Edited by D.A. Thangasamy. Madras: CLS, 1966.

_____. "Kingdom of God, Church and Ashrams," in *Ashrams Past and Present*. Madras: CLS, 1941; reprint, 1996.

_____. *Rethinking Christianity in India*. Edited by Devasahayam, D.M and A.N. Sudarisanam. Madras: Hogarth Press, 1939.

Cobb, John B. Jr. and David Ray Griffin. *Process Theology: An Introductory Exposition* Belfast, Ireland: Westminster Press, 1976.

Cohen, Anthony. *The Symbolic Construction of Community*. Chichester: Harwood, 1985.

Conger, Yves. *I Believe in the Holy Spirit*. New York: Crossroad Herder, 1997.

Cogar Yves. *Lay People in the Church: A Study for a Theology of Laity*. Westminster, MD: Newman, 1965).

Cross F.L. ed. *The Oxford Dictionary of the Christian Church*. New York: Oxford University Press, 1957 reprint 1961.

Das, Bhagwan. "Dalits and the Caste System" in *Indigenous People: Dalits*. Edited by James Massey. Delhi: ISPCK, 1994.

Desroachers, John. *Towards a New India*. Bangalore: CSA, 1995.

Dietrich, Sozanne De. *The Witnessing Community*. Philadelphia: Westminster Press, 1958.

Dietrich, Gabriele and Bas Wielenga. *Towards Understanding Indian Society*. Madurai: Tamilnadu Theological Seminary, 1997.

Dupuis Jacques and Neuner eds. *The Christian Faith*. Bangalore: Theological Publication of India, 1978.

Eliade, Mircea ed., *The Encyclopedia of Religion*, 12. New York: Macmillan, 1989.

Estep, William R. *Renaissance and Reformation*. Michigan: William Eerdmans Publishing Company, 1986.

Fabry, H. "Yahad" in *Theological Dictionary of the Old Testament*. Edited by G. Johannes Botterweck and Helmer Riggen. Translated by David E. Green. Grand Rapids, Michigan: W.M.B. Eerdmans, 1990.

Fiorenza, Elizabeth Schussler. *In Memory of Her: A Feminist Reconstruction of Christian Origins*. New York: Crossroad, 1984.

_____. *Discipleship of Equals: Critical Feminist Ecclesiology for Liberation*. New York: Crossroad, 1993.

Fretheim, Terence. *The Pentateuch*. Nashville: Abingdon Press, 1996.

Fuellenbach, John. *Church: Community for the Kingdom*. Maryknoll, NY: Orbis Books, 2002.

Giner, Salvador. *Sociology*. London: Martin Robertson, 1972.

Gonzalez, Justo L. *A History of Christian Thought*, Vol. 3. Nashville: Abingdon Press, 1975.

Grenz, Stanley J. and Roger E. Olson, *20th Century Theology*. Secunderabad: OM Books, 2004.

Gregorios, Paulos Mar. *A Human God*. Kottayam: Mar Gregorios Foundation, 1992.

_____. *Inter Church Dialogue*. Delhi: ISPCK/MGF, 2010.

Gritsch, Eric W. and Robert W. Jenson. *Lutheranism: The Theological Movement and its Confessional Writings*. Philadelphia: Fortress Press, 1976.

Guthrie, Donald. *The New Testament Theology*. London: IVP, 1981.

Hall, Donald E. *Subjectivity*. New York: Routledge, 1960.

Hanson, Paul D. *The People Called: The Growth of Community in the Bible*. San Francisco: Harper and Row, 1985.

Harvey, Peter. *An Introduction to Buddhism: Teachings, History and Practices*. Cambridge: University Press, 1997.

Hill, Edmund. "Church" in *The New Dictionary of Theology*. Edited by Joseph A. Komonchak, Mary Collins and Dermot A. Lane. Bangalore: Theological Publication of India, 1996.

Harkness, Georgia. *Mysticism: Its Meaning and Message*. Nashville: Abingdon Press, 1953.

Imchen, Panger. *Ancient Ao Naga Religion and Culture*. Delhi: Har-Anand, 1993.

Jay, Eric G. *The Church: Its Changing Image through Twenty Centuries*, Vol. *The First Sixteen Centuries*. London: SPCK, 1977.

Jesson, Nicholas A. *Orthodox Contribution to Ecumenical Ecclesiology*. Toronto: University of St. Michael's College, 2001.

Kappen, Sebastian. *Jesus and Cultural Revolution: An Asian Perspective*. Bombay: Build Publications, 1983.

————. *Jesus and Freedom*. Mary knoll: Orbis, 1977.

Karkainnen, Veli Matti. *An Introduction to Ecclesiology*. Illinois: Intervarsity Press, 2002.

Kasper, Walter. *Theology and Church*. New York: Crossroads, 1989.

Kelly, J.N.D. *Early Christian Doctrines*. New York: Harpers Collins Publishers, 1978.

Kreiss, Wilbert. *History of the Reformation*. Translated by Theodore Mueller. USA: LCMS, 1998.

Lane, Tony. *The Lion Book of Christian Thought*. Tiruvalla: Suvartha Bhavan, 1999.

Lalrinawma, V.S. *Major Faith Traditions of India*. Delhi: ISPCK, 2007.

Lawler, Michael and Thomas J. Shanahan. *Church: A Spiritual Communion*. Collegeville, Minnesota: Liturgical Press, 1995.

Leith, John H. "Ecclesiology," in *A Handbook of Christian Theology*. Edited by Donald W. Musser and Joseph L. Prince. Nashville: Abingdon Press, 1992.

Light Donald et.al., eds. *Reading and Review for Sociology*. New York: McGraw-Hill, 1989.

Livingston, Herbert. *The Pentateuch in its Cultural Environment*. Grand Rapids: Baker, 1987.

Luther, Martin. "On the Councils and the Churches," translated by C.M. Jacobs in *Works of Martin Luther* with Introduction and notes, Vol. V. Philadelphia: Muhlenberg Press, 1931.

Madan, G.R. *Theoretical Sociology*. New Delhi: Mittal publications, 1991.

Massey, James. *Down Trodden: The Struggles of India's Dalits For Identity, Solidarity and Liberation.* Geneva: WCC Publications, 1997.

Martens, Elmer A. *God's Design: A Focus on Old Testament Theology.* Grand Rapids: Baker, 1987.

Martin, James P. "The Church in Mathew," in *Interpreting the Gospels.* Edited by James Luther Mays. Philadelphia: Fortress Press, 1981.

Mcbrien, Richard P. "Church," in *A New Dictionary of Christian Theology.* Edited by Alan Richardson and John Bowden. London: SCM Press Ltd, 1983.

McIver, R.M. and C.H. Page. *Society- An Introductory Analysis,* 1950.

Meeks, M. Douglas. *Origins of the Theology of Hope.* Philadelphia: Fortress, 1974.

Meier, John P. *A Marginal Jew: Rethinking the Historical Jesus.* New York: Doubleday, 2001.

Messner, J. "Community" in *New Catholic Encyclopedia,* Vol. 4. New York: McGraw-Hill Book Company, 1967.

Michael, S.M. "Cultural Studies and Theologizing on the Empowerment of Dalits in India" in *Frontiers in Dalit Hermeneutics.* Edited by James Massey and Samson Prabhakar. Bangalore: BTESSC/SATHRI, 2005.

Morton, T. Ralph. *Community of Faith.* New York: Association Press, 1954.

Mowinkel, Sigmund. *The Psalms in Israel's Worship.* New York: Abingdon Press, 1962.

Muller, H.P. "Qahal," *Theological Lexicon of the Old Testament.* Edited by Ernst Jenni and Claus Westermann, translated by Mark E. Biddle. Massachusetts: Hendrickson, 1997.

Mukherjee, Radhakamal. *The Community of Communities.* Bombay: Manaktalas, 1966.

Newbigin, Leslie. *The Household of God: Lectures on the Nature of the Church.* London: SCM press, 1953.

Pannenberg, Wolfhart. *Systematic Theology* Vol. 3, translated by Geoffrey W. Bromiley. Michigan: William Eerdmans Publishing Company, 1998.

_____. *The Church,* translated by Keith Crim. Philadelphia: Westminster Press, 1983.

Pathil, Kuncheria. *Theology of the Church New Horizon.* Bangalore: Dharmaram Publications, 2006.

Rahner, Karl. "Observations of the Factor of the Charismatic in the Church," in *Theological Investigations XII.* New York: Seabury, 1974.

Ramakrishnan, Venkitesh. "Swami's Confession," in *Frontline.* Vol. 28 No. 3, February 11, 2011.

Rapport, Nigel and Joanna Overing. *Key Concepts in Social and Cultural Anthropology.* New York: Routledge, 2004.

Rasmusson, Arne. *The Church as Polis: From Political Theology to Theological Politics as Exemplified by Jurgen Moltmann and Stanley Hauerwas.* Lund: Lund University Press, 1994.

Rawat, H.K. *Sociology: Basic Concepts.* New Delhi: Rawat Publications, 2007.

Rawls, John. *The Theory of Justice.* London: Harvard University Press, 1971.

Redfield, Robert. *The Little Community and Peasant Society and Culture.* Chicago: University of Chicago Press, 1960.

Remmling, Gunter and Robert B. Campbell. *Basic Sociology: An Introduction to the Study of Society.* New Jersey: Littlefield Adams, 1976.

Robinson, J.A.T. *The Body: A Study in Pauline Theology.* London: SCM Press, 1963.

Rouse, Ruth. *A History of the Ecumenical Movement 1517-1948.* Edited by Stephen Neil. Geneva: WCC, 1989.

Russell, Letty. *Church in the Round: Feminist Interpretation of the Church.* Louisville: Westminster John Knox, 1993.

Sabanes, Julio R. "Biblical Understanding of Community" in *Man in Community: Christian Concern for the Human in Changing Society.* Edited by Egbert De Vries. New York: Association, 1966.

Sagorsky, Nicholas. *Ecumenism, Christian Origins and the Practice of Communion.* Cambridge: University Press, 2000.

Schmidt, K.L. "Ekklesia," in *Theological Dictionary of the New Testament.* Edited by Gerhard Kittel, translated by Geoffrey Bromiley Vol. 3. Michigan: Eerdmans Publishing Company, 1965, Reprint 1976.

Schnore, Leo. F. *"Community"* in *Sociology: An Introduction,* edited by Neil J. Smelser. New Delhi: Wiley Eastern, 1970.

Schwarz, Hans. *The Christian Church.* Minneapolis: Augsburg: Publishing House, 1982.

Scott, Corinne. "The Context for Feminist Theologizing: Violence Against Women/ Women Against Violence" in *Feminist Theology: Perspectives and Praxis.* Edited by Prasanna Kumari. Chennai: Gurukul Lutheran Theological College and Research Institute,1999.

Shults, F. Leron. *Reforming Theological Anthropology: After the Philosophical Turn to Relationality.* Michigan: W.B. Eerdmans, 2003.

Sills, David L. ed. *International Encyclopedia of the Social Sciences,* Vol. 3. London: MacMillan, 1972.

Stanislaus, L. *The Liberative Mission of the Church among Dalit Christians.* Delhi: ISPCK, 1999.

Stephen, Abraham. "Christ and Culture: An Examination of M.M. Thomas' Theology of Religions" in *Contextualization: A Re-reading of M.M. Thomas.* Edited by Godwin Shiri. Tiruvalla: Christava Sahitya Samithi, 2007.

Theissen, Gerd. *The First Followers of Jesus.* London: SCM Press, 1978.

Thanzauva, K. *Theology of Community: Tribal Theology in the Making.* Aizwal: Academy of Integrated Christian Studies, 2004.

Thatcher, O.J. and E.H. Mc Neal. *A Source Book for Medieval History.* New York: Harper and Row Publishers, 1905.

Thomas, M.M. "The Struggle for Human Dignity as a Preparation for the Gospel" in *Renewal for Mission.* Edited by Lyon and Manuel. Madras: CLS, 1976.

_____. *The Gospel of Forgiveness and Koinonia.* Delhi: ISPCK and Thiruvalla: CSS, 1994.

_____. *Salvation and Humanization: Some Crucial Issues of the Theology of Mission in Contemporary India.* Madras: CLS, 1971.

_____. *Towards a Theology of Contemporary Ecumenism.* Madras: CLS, 1970.

_____. *Some Theological Dialogues.* Madras: CLS, 1977.

_____. *Risking Christ for Christ's Sake: Towards an Ecumenical Theology of Pluralism.* Geneva: WCC, Publications, 1987.

_____. Newbigin. "Salvation and Humanization: A Discussion" in *Mission Trends,* No.1, 1974.

Tillich, Paul. *A Complete History of Christian Thought.* Edited by Carl E. Braaten. New York: Harper and Row Publishers, 1968.

Varghese, Mathew. *An Appraisal of the Concept of Community in the Writings of Leonardo Boff and Select Indian Christian Theologians to Develop a Theology of the Community' in the Indian Context,* A Dissertation Submitted to the Senate of Serampore College for the Degree of Doctor of Theology, 2004.

Van Der Ven, Johannes A. *Ecclesiology in Context.* Grand Rapids: William E.B. Eerdmans, 1993.

Vandervelde, George. "Koinonia Ecclesiology: Ecumenical Breakthrough," in *One in Christ* 29, 1993.

Varghese, Paul. *The Church in India: Where We Headed.* An Unpublished article dated 24.8.1973.

Vashum, Yanghkahao. "Towards a Tribal Theology of Eco-Human Rights: Resources from the Tangkhul Tradition." in *Journal of Tribal Studies* 3/1 January-June 1999.

Volf, Miroslav. *The Church as the Image of the Trinity.* Grand Rapids: Eerdmans Publishing Company, 1998.

Wall, Robert W. "Community" in *Anchor Bible Dictionary.* Edited by David Noel Freedman. Vol.1 New York: Doubleday, 1992.

Walker, G.S.M. "Church," *New Bible Dictionary,* 2nd edition. Secunderabad : OM, 1990, reprint 1993.

Walker. Williston. *A History of the Christian Church,* 4th edition. Edinburgh: T&T Clark Ltd., 1986.

Ware, Kallistos. *The Orthodox Church,* revised edition. London: Penguin, 1993.

_____. *The Orthodox Way*. New York: St. Vladimir's Seminary Press, 1999.

Wielengen, Bastiaan. "With Nagas found in Different Society" in *Christian Witness in Society*, edited by K.C. Abraham. Bangalore: BTE-SSC, 1998.

Westhelle, *Vitor. The Church Event: Call and Challenge of a Church Protestant*. Minneapolis: Fortress Press, 2010.

Yamunacharya, M. *Ramanuja's Teachings in his own Words*. Bombay: Bharatiya Vidya Bhavan, 1970.

Zizioulas, John D. *Being as Communion: Studies in Personhood and Church*. New York: St. Vladimir Seminary, 1985.

"Religion, Community and Society" in *The Encyclopedia of Religions*, 1987.

"Sangha and Society," in *The Encyclopedia of Religion*, Vol. 13. Edited by Miercea Eliade. New York: MacMillan, 1987.

"Ummah" *The Oxford Encyclopedia of the Modern Islamic World* Vol. 4. Edited by John L. Esposito. New York: Oxford University, 1995.

"Ummah" in *The Encyclopedia of Religions*, 123.

# Articles in Journals, Periodicals and Newspapers

Ali Engineer, Ashgar. "2010- Year of Communal Riots," in *Indian Currents*, Vol. 23, No.2, December 2010.

Dabhi, Jimmy. "Dalit Human Rights: Issues and Perspectives," *Social Action* Vol. 24/No. 1, January-March 2004.

David, James. "Special Economic Zones," in *Integral Liberation*. Vol. 2/ No. 3, September 2007.

D'souza, Simon Paul. "India at Sixty" in *Integral Liberation*. Vol. 2/No. 3, September 2007.

Hemrom, A.S. "The Role of Churches in building up Adivasi Solidarity: The Call for an Ecumenical Task," *NCC Review* Vol. CXXX/No. 2, February 2004.

Hiddleston, Sarah. "Poisoned" in *Frontline*, Sept. 24, 2010.

Hooft, W.A. Visser't. "The Basis: Its History and Significance," in *Ecumenical Review* 2, 1985.

Kanichai, Cyriac. "Satsang vis-à-vis Community Life" in *Third Millennium* ¾ April 2000.

John, T.A. "Gender Equality: Chasing a Millennium Goal for the Long Haul," in *Social Action*. Vol. 57/ No. 2, April- June 2007.

Kullu, Paulus "Tribal Spirituality: An Integrated Life with Belief," *Sevartham* 21, 1996.

Lobo, Lancy. "Communalism and Christian Response in India" in *Vidyajyoti Journal of Theological Reflection*. Vol. LIX/ No.6, June 1995.

Mitra, N.B. "Bishops Condemn Government Assault on Minority Rights," in *People's Reporter* Vol. 20/ No. 3, Feb 10-25, 2007.

Moses, Y. "Peoples' Politics and the role of Indian Church," in *NCC Review* Vol. CXXVI/ No. 10, Nov 2006.

Puniyani, Ram. "Common Minimum Program and Outcome of Secularism" in *Social Action* Vol. LIV/No.3, July-September 2006.

Radha Krishnan, M.G. "Ire of the Minorities," in *India Today* Vol. XXXIII/No.1, Jan 1-7, 2008.

Rebeiro, M. "Origin of the Church," in *Living Word* 3/13. May-June 1989.

Soares-Prabhu, George M. "Radical Beginnings: The Jesus Community as the Archetype of the Church," *Jeevadhara*, Vol. XV, No. 88, 1985.

Sukhadeo Thorat Committee Report: Caste Discrimination in AIIMS," *Economic and Political Weekly* Vol. XLII/ No. 22, June 2-8, 2007.

Thomas M.M. "Christ-centered Syncretism" in *Religion and Society*, December 21, 1974.

Tripathi, Purnima S. "Offence as Defense" in *Frontline*. Vol. 28 No. 3, February 11, 2011.

Wilfred, Felix. "Subaltern and Ethical Auditing," *Jeevadhara* Vol. XXXVII/No. 217, January 2007.

*Indian Express,* 22 September 2010.

*The Hindu* (Kerala), 22 September 2010.

*The Hindu* (Kerala), 19 September 2010.

www.ingramcontent.com/pod-product-compliance
Lightning Source LLC
Chambersburg PA
CBHW031202260626
47169CB00004B/1218